★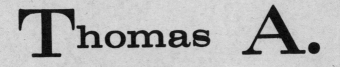

Thomas A. Edison

Young Inventor

Illustrated by Wallace Wood

Thomas A. Edison

Young Inventor

By Sue Guthridge

Aladdin Paperbacks

Aladdin Paperbacks
An imprint of Simon & Schuster
Children's Publishing Division
1230 Avenue of the Americas
New York, New York 10020
Text copyright © 1947, 1959 by the Bobbs-Merrill Co., Inc.

First Aladdin Paperbacks edition, 1986
Manufactured in the United States of America

20
Library of Congress Cataloging-in-Publication Data

Guthridge, Sue, 1918-
    Thomas A. Edison, young inventor.

    Reprint. Originally published: Indianapolis : Bobbs-
Merrill, 1947.
    Summary: A biography focusing on the childhood of
the inventor who patented more than 1,100 inventions in
sixty years, among them the electric light and the
phonograph.
    1. Edison, Thomas A. (Thomas Alva), 1847-1931—
Juvenile literature.   2. Inventors—United States—
Biography—Juvenile literature.   3. Kentucky—Biography
—Juvenile literature.   [1. Edison, Thomas A.
(Thomas Alva), 1847-1931.   2. Inventors]   I. Title.
TK140.E3G9   1986   621.3'092'4 [B] [92]   86-10862
ISBN 0-02-041850-7

To my mother

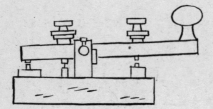

Illustrations

Full pages

Numerous smaller illustrations

Contents

★ ★ Thomas A. Edison

Young Inventor

An Idea That Didn't Work

"Tom Edison, where are you going with all those biscuits? And I wondered what had happened to that slice of ham. Tom, where are you going now?"

"I've got another idea, Mother. I want to try it out. I'm going to the henhouse."

Six-year-old Tom hurried out to the little white frame henhouse built behind the red brick house. He stood on the little hill that overlooked the Huron River. It was bordered by a narrow towpath. As he looked up the river he could see the little houses of Milan, Ohio, nestling on the riverbank. A crisp breeze was blowing.

In the distance he could see the Milan ship-yards. For a minute Tom watched a barge. It was slowly making its way to the canal which would take it out into Lake Erie. The barge had a long rope attached to it. The other end of the rope was fastened to the harness of a mule which was plodding along the towpath.

The boat was loaded, Tom noticed, with fresh-ly sawed lumber. It carried a lot of coal, too. Maybe, thought Tom, the barge had traded this load for iron stoves and tinware. Sometimes the barges brought in bright-colored silk and mus-lin, or tea and coffee and spices.

When the barge reached the canal there would be a change, Tom knew. Its load would be taken off and put on a river boat pulled by horses. Then the river boat would go out into Lake Erie, and the passengers would get on steamboats. They would stop at many exciting towns. Detroit would be an important stop.

Maybe they would go as far east as Buffalo or even New York City.

Tom pulled at his right eyebrow and shook his blond hair out of his eyes. Suddenly he remembered his idea. He clutched his package of biscuits and his slice of ham tighter and started to run toward the henhouse.

Inside the little building it wasn't very light. Tom could feel the hens and the chickens bump against his legs as they hurried to get out of his way. At first he could not see them, but soon his eyes became used to the darkness. He found Lulu's nest over in the far corner. Lulu was Tom's pet goose. She was sitting quietly on her nest when Tom went up to her.

"Lulu, you must get off that nest now. You've been there for four weeks, and I haven't seen any baby geese yet. I'm tired of waiting. Now get off!"

With much hissing and scolding at her master,

Lulu scurried off her nest. Tom took off his coat and cap and reached up to hang them on a nail. He wasn't very tall, and he had to stand on his very tiptoes to put his cap on top of his coat. He placed the biscuits and ham by the side of the nest before he examined the six big white eggs. Then he cautiously climbed to the box in which Lulu had been sitting. He sat down very carefully on the eggs.

After a while it seemed to Tom that he had been sitting long enough to hatch at least one. He got off the nest with great care. All six eggs were just as they had been. Tom looked at Lulu who had just waddled into the henhouse.

"Not yet, Lulu. But don't worry. I won't break your eggs. I'm not really big enough. The men I know at the shipyard say I'm skinny. A skinny boy couldn't break your eggs."

As Tom sat down again, Lulu turned around and went out into the chicken yard. Several

times during the afternoon Tom got off the nest and looked at the eggs. They hadn't hatched yet.

Mrs. Edison was busy in her cheery kitchen. It was time to start supper. The teakettle was already singing as it swung from its crane over the fire in the large stone fireplace.

"Samuel," Mrs. Edison called to Tom's father, "will you please go down to the cellar for me? I need some potatoes. By the way, have you seen Tom this afternoon?"

"Nancy, I haven't been near this house since lunchtime. I didn't see him around the lumber-yard. I had to take old Mr. Barnaby some new shingles for his barn roof. He says the folks here won't let the railroad run its tracks through this town. Why, he says——"

"Samuel, I'm not interested in any railroad tracks coming through my front yard. I *am* interested in potatoes and in knowing where Tom is. I need wood for this stove. If we are going to have side meat and hominy tonight, I have to have more wood," said Mrs. Edison.

"I'll get the wood for you after I get the potatoes."

"No, that's Tom's work. It's high time he was in here helping me, but he went off with another of his ideas. I declare, Tom is fuller of ideas than this woodbox is of wood. Where *is* that boy?"

Tom's mother turned from the kitchen table and went to the back door. She called, "Tom! Tom Edison, come here at once!"

There was no answer. Mrs. Edison went out to the hillside behind the house. Again she called, "Thomas Alva Edison, come here at once!"

And still there was no answer. Mrs. Edison put her shawl over her head and started toward the henhouse. She shooed the chickens out of her way and opened the door with a quick jerk.

What she saw made her stop in the doorway.

17

Then she laughed. "Tom Edison!" she exclaimed. "What are you doing? Why are you sitting on Lulu's nest?"

"I am bigger than Lulu, Mother, and I should be warmer. If I *am* bigger and warmer then I ought to be able to hatch her eggs quicker than she does. She takes too long. She's been here for four weeks now."

"Tom, Tom," his mother said, laughing so hard she had to wipe the tears from her eyes with the corner of her shawl. "You are much, much heavier than Lulu. Those eggs must all be broken."

"Oh, no, Mother, I looked. I'm sitting on them as easily as Lulu does."

"But Tom, would you want to sit out here on a nest for days? Hadn't you better leave that work to Lulu?"

"I *am* a little hungry," Tom admitted.

"Didn't I see you go out with some biscuits

18

and ham?" asked Mrs. Edison, with a twinkle in her eyes.

"I thought it might take longer than just this afternoon. But I've already eaten the ham and biscuits."

"Well," Mrs. Edison said, still laughing, "get your cap and your coat and come in to supper. I need you to get some wood for me. There's Lulu, Tom," she added as she went out into the chicken yard. "You'd better put her back on her nest."

Tom started toward the henhouse door. Just then Lulu came in and hurried over to her box. She got up on her nest and turned the eggs over very carefully.

"They're all there, Lulu. I didn't break any of them."

Lulu seemed satisfied with what Tom had told her. She settled down once more to the long task of hatching her own eggs.

Tom Visits the Shipyards

"SEE WHERE I was standing, Mr. Anderson? Way back there? Well, then, why could I see that hammer in your hand hit the board before I could hear it?"

Mr. Anderson sat back on his heels at the side of the barge he was working on. Tom could look over Mr. Anderson's shoulder and see the Huron River in the distance. The canal beyond it was covered with ice now.

"Ever been out in a storm, Tom?" asked Mr. Anderson, in answer to Tom's question.

"Sure, and I'm not scared of them, either, Mr. Anderson," Tom told him with a brave look.

"Well, then, Master Tom, answer me this. Do you hear the thunder first or do you see the lightning first?"

Tom watched Mr. Anderson hammer the last floor board on the bottom of the barge. He pulled at his right eyebrow and thought for a full minute.

"I see the lightning first. And then I count slowly and stop when I hear the thunder."

"That's right, Tom. And it's practically the same with this hammer. You see, light travels pretty fast, and you see by that light. It goes much faster than sound can go. Now you run back there about where Sandy is sitting and we'll try it again. As soon as you see the hammer fall on this board you start counting. Count the way you do when you see lightning flash. As soon as you can hear the hammer fall, stop counting. Is that clear?"

"Oh, yes, Mr. Anderson," said Tom, excitedly.

21

He ran over to where a large man with red hair was sitting. He was putting some kind of black stuff on the bottom of a small barge.

"Hello there, Sandy," Tom called, as he came up to his best friend at the shipyard.

"Hello, Tom. Haven't seen you for about two days. Did you run out of questions?"

"No, Sandy, not that. I've just been busy, I guess. Mr. Anderson and I are experimenting again. Watch."

Sandy dropped his heavy brush and stood up, all attention. He always liked to tease Tom about his questions. And he was always interested in Tom's experiments.

Tom put his hands to his mouth and called, "Are you ready, Mr. Anderson?" He turned his head so that he would be sure to hear the answer. Mr. Anderson was so far away that Tom could not see his face clearly.

Then came the answer: "I'm ready, Master

Tom. I'm ready. Now you be sure to watch the hammer closely."

Tom and Sandy both watched the hammer. Mr. Anderson, thought Tom, must be counting, *one-two-three*. Then the hammer fell.

Tom started counting, *one-two*—— The sound of metal striking hard wood came to his ears. Tom took hold of Sandy's hand, and away they ran to Mr. Anderson.

"It took two! It took two!" Tom shouted.

"Do you understand why you saw the hammer hit the wood before you heard it?" Mr. Anderson asked Tom.

"I understand now. That was fun," he told the boatbuilder.

Then he asked, "Sandy, what was that black stuff in the bucket you were painting with?"

"That's pitch, Tom."

"What is pitch, Sandy?"

Before Sandy could answer again, an old man who was helping him brought his head up with a jerk. "Tom, you're one of my favorite boys, but you ask so many questions! Maybe it would save time for us if we'd hire a man just to answer them for you!"

"I wish you would, Mr. Thornton," Tom told him. "I wish you would."

"Tom, look over yonder," said Mr. Anderson. "Isn't that Pitt coming at a fast pace? It appears to me he might be looking for one small brother. And he seems to be excited about something, doesn't he?"

"Pitt! Here I am. Over by Mr. Anderson."

"We've been looking all over for you, Tom," said Pitt, panting from his long run. "The most wonderful thing is about to happen!"

"What's going to happen?" asked Tom.

"You'd never guess, so I'll have to tell you. We're going to move away from Milan!"

"Oh, Pitt!" cried Tom. "You mean we're going to take a trip? On one of those iron engines on the railroad?"

"You mean you're going to take our Mr. Question Box away from us?" asked Mr. Anderson.

"I'm afraid so, Mr. Anderson. You see, the new railroad is going *past* Milan instead of through the town, and that will take away a lot of our business."

"Yes, Pitt, it will. People won't be coming here to buy the things they need."

"When are we going?" asked Tom. "What kind of house will we have? Will Tannie come and see us often? What——"

"Wait a minute, Tom. Not so fast." Pitt laughed.

"You'll get like us, Master Pitt," said Sandy. "Just listen to 'em all and then answer what you can. Let the rest of them fade into the blue."

"Come on, now, Tom. We'll tell you all about the trip and the new house," said Pitt.

When the boys got home they found Mr. and Mrs. Edison talking in the parlor.

"Pitt has heard that there is money to be made in the grain and feed business up in Michigan," Mr. Edison was saying. He puffed on his pipe.

"We could leave Milan and travel to Detroit, Michigan, by railroad. Then we could go by steamboat from Detroit across Lake St. Clair and settle somewhere along the St. Clair River in Michigan.

26

"There is a lot of lumber up in those parts, too. I could run a lumber business on the side," he added.

"Land of goodness, Samuel! You mean I should suddenly pick up and leave Milan, after we've lived here so long? Why, it's been fifteen years since we came here with three little children. Now Pitt is twenty-one. Marion is married. Tannie will soon marry and leave us. Tom is getting to be a big boy. He's almost seven."

"Yes, and I can still remember how cold it was that morning in February when he was born. That was February 11, 1847. Why, Nancy, next week is Tom's birthday! I had almost forgotten about it."

"What do you want for your birthday, son?" asked Tom's mother.

"I want a hickory-nut cake with burnt-sugar icing," Tom said.

Mr. Edison was still thinking about business.

"Nancy," he said, "I am sorry, but I feel that we will have to move."

Tom's gray eyes grew bright with excitement. Imagine, a trip on a train and on a boat!

Mrs. Edison was the only one who did not want to move.

"Here Pitt is old enough to have a business of his own," she said. "Marion is married to a fine young man. She lives close enough so that she can come to see us often. It is time for Tom to begin school. And now you want me to pick up and leave. Just because of a railroad."

"But, Nancy, you can see that this new-fangled contraption is going to ruin our business in Milan."

"What is a 'new-fangled contraption'?" asked Tom.

"That is what the men in town call the railroad, Tom," said Mr. Edison.

"I thought," sighed Mrs. Edison, "that I'd

never forget the year 1828 when we were married. Now I wager I'll never forget 1854! First it's a 'new-fangled contraption' coming down the road, puffing and panting. Then it goes right past Milan and everyone's business is ruined. Then the Edison family has to move way up into Michigan. And all because the 'new-fangled contraption' didn't come through the town!"

"It's the truth, Nancy. More and more of the businessmen are leaving. This will soon be a ghost town. I want to leave before that."

"What is a ghost town, Father?" asked Tom

"It is a town, Tom, that used to have people and animals, but for some reason they all left. The old houses and buildings are empty and boarded up. It looks as if only ghosts might live there."

Tom sprang up. "When do we go, Father?" he asked excitedly.

Before Mr. Edison could answer Tom's question his mother asked, "Where *is* this place you want us to go, Pitt?"

"It's about fifty miles northeast of Detroit, on the St. Clair River."

"*What* is on the St. Clair River?" Tom asked.

"The town, Tom. Port Huron, Michigan."

"Port Huron, Michigan," whispered Tom to himself. It sounded strange and exciting.

"Tom," said Pitt, "this beats any of your ideas, doesn't it?"

"Oh, yes, Pitt. I can hardly wait to go. Shall I get ready now? May I take Lulu? What about the cow? Will we leave the chickens?"

"Tom! Tom!" laughed his mother. "One question at a time, please. We won't move for a few weeks yet. You'll have one more birthday in Milan."

A Birthday to Remember

WHEN Tom first woke up he knew it must be fairly early in the morning. He could just see the light coming in at the top of each windowpane. The rest of the glass was frosted with a thin coat of ice. He put his head under the heavy comforts again for one last little snooze before he had to jump out of bed.

"Tom!" he heard his mother call from the kitchen below his room. "Tom, it's time to get up. Hurry, and dress down here because your room is bound to be cold."

"Yes, Mother," came a muffled sound from under the covers. And then he was out of bed.

He ran over to the window. With his warm fingers he rubbed a spot on the glass so he could look out. It was a clear cold morning, just right for ice skating, he thought. That exciting idea made him dash to the pitcher of water on the washstand in a hurry.

Tom broke the thin layer of ice which had formed in the pitcher and poured some water into the bowl. Then he splashed his face and hands and wiped them faster than he could count to ten. He grabbed his clothes and ran down the stairs and into the bright kitchen.

"Good morning, Mother," Tom said as he ran over to give her a hug. "It feels nice and warm here in the kitchen by the fire."

After Tom had dressed, his mother said, "Do you know what day this is?"

"Well, it must be—why, it's February eleventh, of course! It's my birthday!"

"And may you have a happy one, too, Tom,"

his mother said. "But now come and eat your breakfast."

Tom went over to the table and started to sit down, but forgot all about eating when he saw three packages at his place. He picked up the largest one of all. It was long and narrow and rather deep. As he untied the string, Pitt came bounding into the kitchen.

"Happy birthday, Tom! Pretty soon you're going to be as old as your brother. Right?" said Pitt, slapping Tom on the back.

"And I'll be glad, too," Tom told Pitt, as he excitedly wadded up the string and paper.

Mr. Edison came into the room just in time to watch Tom's face as he opened the box. "A happy birthday, my boy! Do you like them?"

"Oh, Father, *new* ice skates! New ice skates! And today is just the kind of day to use them. Oh, thank you, thank you, Mother and Father."

He sat down immediately and tried the skates on. "Look," he cried, "they fit exactly!"

"What about those other packages I see on the table?" Pitt reminded him.

Tom took the skates off and ran back to the table to unwrap the other two packages. One was a set of colored pencils and the other was a large pad of sketching paper.

"I was talking to Sandy the other day, Tom. He told me you go to the square almost every day and copy the signs on the buildings. Now you can copy the names of the boats we pass on the way to Port Huron," said Pitt. "And there should be lots of signs."

"Thank you, Pitt. These are wonderful!" said Tom, as he tried every one of the colors on the first page of the sketching pad.

"Why do you copy the signs, Tom?" his father asked.

"I do it to learn my letters. I can spell 'blacksmith' now, and 'lumber' and even 'grain elevator,' " Tom told his father.

"Blacksmith?" asked Pitt. "Let's hear you spell it now."

"All right," said Tom. "B-l-a-c-k-s-m-i-t-h."

"Not bad for a boy who just this very day turned seven," remarked his father. "But I'm hungry and I smell biscuits. Let's eat and then Tom can go out and try his skates. That is, after he feeds the chickens and the geese."

And biscuits there were, with honey from the Edisons' own beehives to pour over them. There were fried ham and potatoes and milk so rich that little flecks of golden cream floated on the top of Tom's glass.

"For such a little boy, Tom, you can stow away more food than anyone I know," Pitt said, after they had finished eating.

"I'm not so little, Pitt. Look." Tom stood and pulled himself up as straight as he could, but still he didn't look very tall. He put on his coat and wrapped a muffler around his neck. Then he pulled the stocking cap his mother had knit for him well over his ears. He started for the cellar to get the feed for the chickens.

"Tom, didn't I hear you tell me once that you wanted a hickory-nut cake for your birthday?" asked Mrs. Edison.

"Oh, yes, Mother. Shall I get the nuts while I'm in the cellar?" he asked.

"That's exactly right, son. Make the one trip do for the two things."

Soon Tom had brought the hickory nuts to his mother. He fed the chickens and put fresh water in their pans. Then he ran into the house and picked up his skates. With a quick good-by, he ran off toward the canal.

Tom ran almost all the way, stopping now and then to get his breath, but only for a moment. He was too excited and too eager to try his skates. He had a special place to skate near the ship-yards. It wasn't long until he could see the buildings by the canal.

He went to one of the little shacks where he knew his friend Sandy would be working. "Good morning, Sandy," he said as he pushed open the door of the workshop.

"Good morning to you, Master Tom. Why are you so excited and happy?" Sandy asked.

"It's my birthday and I'm seven and I got a new pair of ice skates," Tom told him all in one breath.

"Well, well, well!" was all Sandy could manage to say.

Tom went over to the stove in the middle of the room and pulled off his mittens to warm his hands. "It's very cold out, Sandy, but just the best kind of day to go skating."

"That's right, Tom," said Sandy. "So you're seven years old today! I guess birthday greetings are in order. Many happy returns, Tom!"

"Thank you, Sandy. Is the ice thick clear across the canal?"

"Let's go see." The two of them went out and walked over to the edge of the canal.

"Looks pretty good to me, Tom," said Sandy. "But wait a minute. See that spot over yonder that is lighter than the rest? You'd better not get too near that. There aren't many of us here working today, and I'd feel more comfortable if you stayed closer to the edge."

"I see it. But why does it look lighter than the rest of the canal?" Tom asked.

"Because, Tom, the ice is so thin there that you can see the water underneath. Now don't you go near it," Sandy cautioned him again.

Tom sat down on a log, and Sandy helped him fasten his skate straps.

"Now you're all ready, and a prettier pair of birthday skates I've never seen," Sandy said. "Watch out for that spot. When you get cold come in and warm yourself at the stove. I'll look out the window every now and then and keep my eye on you. Your mother would never forgive me if I didn't."

Tom crossed over to the edge of the canal and stepped onto the ice. He skated carefully for a while, trying the ice to be certain it was safe enough. Sandy stood and watched him. Then, sure that Tom was going to be all right, he went back into the warm shack.

Tom thought he never had been so happy before in all his life. It was wonderful to skim lightly across the ice. He kept close to the shore. He skated up and down, singing at the top of his voice all the songs he could remember. Then he tried to do figure eights, but he didn't seem to have enough room.

He sat down at the edge of the canal to tighten the straps before going on. He looked up into the bare branches of a tree on the bank. There was a lone sparrow sitting on one of the limbs watching him.

40

"Poor Mr. Sparrow! Aren't you sorry you can't skate the way I can?" Tom asked the bird. But the sparrow didn't seem to be too sorry, for he said nothing.

"I think, Mr. Sparrow," said Tom, "that I'll go out a little farther where I will have more room to do a figure eight."

Tom started out toward the middle of the canal. After several long glides he began to make a beautiful figure eight. It was great fun, but he didn't have quite enough space to finish the eight. He skated back toward the bank, going faster and faster all the time.

Finally he got to the center of the canal and made a giant circle for the bottom of the eight. Then he started to make another circle which would be the top of the eight. Just as he got to the top and was ready to turn and come back to meet the first circle he heard a frightening noise.

Before Tom knew what happened he was

completely surrounded by water! He reached out for the edge of the ice. But each time he tried to hold fast to it and pull himself out, the ice broke off and floated on the water. Then Tom started yelling for Sandy.

"Sandy! Sandy! I fell in. Come get me out. Quick!" he called frantically.

He didn't see Sandy's door open. Suddenly he found an edge of ice which seemed firm, and he was busy holding onto it as hard as he could. Once more he called to his friend, "Sandy, come quick! Sandy!"

And then Tom saw Sandy rush out of his shack. Sandy called, "Hold on, my boy! Hold on! I'll get a piece of rope and be with you in a jiffy."

Tom saw Sandy go back into the shack. Then the old man came out with a length of rope in his hand. He hurried down to the canal and started to run out to Tom, forgetting how slick the ice would be. He slipped and came down so hard

42

that Tom thought surely Sandy, too, would fall through the ice. He looked funny sprawled out. Tom couldn't help laughing, and that made him feel better.

Sandy got to his knees and began to crawl out toward Tom. Little by little he came closer. By this time Tom's hands were so cold he knew he couldn't hold on much longer. His feet were so cold that he could hardly feel them.

"Catch the end of this rope, Tom!" cried Sandy, as it came sailing through the air. But it landed so far away that Tom couldn't possibly reach it.

Sandy pulled the rope back and threw it again. This time it fell right by Tom's left hand. He caught it and held it tightly. "Now what will I do, Sandy?" he called.

"Just hold it, Tom! Hold tight!"

Tom held on with both hands.

"Now," Sandy called, "I'll pull you in."

"All right, Sandy, hurry! I'll try to help as much as I can."

Sandy began to pull on the rope slowly. He watched Tom as the little boy tried to crawl out of the hole. Sandy saw Tom rise little by little until he could put his knees up on the edge of the ice. Then he was out of the hole. Sandy made his way back to the thicker ice, pulling on the rope all the time. And before Tom knew it, Sandy had picked him up in his arms and was carrying him into the shack.

Sandy put Tom, all wrapped up in a blanket, on a chair in front of the stove. He rubbed his hands hard until Tom could feel the blood tingling in them. Then he took off Tom's shoes and skates and rubbed his feet the same way.

"It's a good thing, Tom, that your mother knits such heavy stockings for you. If she didn't, your feet would have been frozen by now. And if you weren't such a mite, I never could have

44

pulled you out of that hole. You're a brave boy for a seven-year-old, too."

"I just watched you all the time, Sandy, and I didn't have time to be scared. But I got awfully cold, and I began to think of the hickory-nut cake that Mother is baking for me and I wished I had a piece. I was afraid I'd lose my skates, too. I saved them, though!"

"I'm glad they didn't come off," Sandy said. "Now I'm going to bundle you up even more and take you home. Bed's the place for you, birthday or no birthday."

"Anyway, it'll be a birthday I won't soon forget," said Tom.

Off for a
New Home

"Now WHERE in the world has Tom gone? Pitt, have you seen your brother since breakfast?" asked Mrs. Edison as she tied the strings of her bonnet under her chin. "Where can he be? It's almost time for Sandy to be here with the wagon. We must be ready."

"Here he comes, Mother," said Pitt. "Tom, don't you know the rest of us are all ready to leave?"

"I'm sorry, but I was busy," Tom answered. "I was—out looking around. It seems so lonesome with all the chickens sold and the cow gone. So lonesome."

47

"Tom, Tom, I declare I don't see how you can get away from us in such a hurry," his mother told him. "Where is your hat? And where is your scarf? Land sakes, one would think to look at you it was June instead of the middle of March! How many times have I told you not to run out of the house without your hat? You'll be having another cold."

"Where is Tannie, Mother?" asked Tom as he began to search for his hat.

"She went up to the attic to see if we forgot anything. I hear her coming down the stairs now," Mrs. Edison said. She was hurrying through the house looking behind all the doors and into all the corners to be sure nothing had been left behind.

"I did find one thing, Mother," said Tannie. She stood in the kitchen doorway with her hands behind her back. She was wearing a dark-green wool coat which buttoned clear down to the floor. On her brown curls was a green bonnet which matched her coat.

"Here's your hat, Tom." Mrs. Edison picked it up from the top of a crate near the fireplace. "And see that you wear it, too."

"Tannie, what do you have in that box?" asked Mr. Edison as he came in from the front of the house. He had been checking over the crates of furniture and other household goods. "What in the world is it?"

"I think it's Tom's, Father," Tannie said. She looked at Tom and winked.

"Oh, Tannie, please give it to me. I know what it is, and do be careful with it, please," cried Tom, running over to where Tannie was standing.

Mrs. Edison looked up. "Why, Tom," she said, "what is in that box? It has holes all over the top."

By this time even Mr. Edison and Pitt had

become interested in what Tannie held behind her back. They stopped moving the crates from the house to the roadside so that they could listen.

"Please, Mother," said Tom, almost in tears, "let me take her. I promise that she won't cause any trouble. I'll keep her with me all the time and you won't even know she is near. Please!"

" 'Please' what, Tom?" asked his mother. "What do you have in that box? Tell me quickly because——"

"Here's Sandy, Mother, and we'll have to hurry!" Pitt said as he rushed into the kitchen to carry out the last of the crates.

In the last-minute excitement of leaving, Tom and his box were completely forgotten by all but two people. Tom looked up at his sister. "Tannie, please don't make me leave her here. Please don't!"

"All right, Tom. You may take Lulu, but I

don't know what Mother will say when she finds out. She may not like it at all. It's going to take us all afternoon and evening to get to Detroit. We will have to stay there all night. Then we will get on the steamboat the next morning, and we'll be on the lake all that day and far into the night. What will you do with Lulu all that time?"

"I'll take good care of her, Tannie. She won't bother anyone at all."

"Tannie! Tom! Hurry! Hurry! We have the wagon packed and Sandy is all ready to go," called Mr. Edison. "Hurry now. You don't want to be left, do you?"

"We're coming, Father," Tannie answered. "Here, Tom," she whispered. "I'll take Lulu and put this lap robe over her. No one would ever guess that I have a goose under this robe. Now come on, let's hurry."

So Tom and his sister Tannie were the last

ones to leave their old home in Milan for a new home in faraway Michigan.

"Good morning, Miss Tannie," said Sandy as he helped her into the wagon.

"Good morning, Sandy," Tannie said. "I still have a lot of work to do fixing up my own new

home, but I couldn't think of letting Mother
move without help from me." Tannie planned to
return to Milan very soon. She would stay with
her sister Marion until she was married. "I'm
looking forward to seeing that country up in
Michigan. I love boat rides, too."

Tom scrambled up on the wagon and sat on the floor at the back, leaning against the long roll of carpeting. "Good-by, Milan," he said. He looked for the last time at the little red brick house on the hillside. Behind it he could see the silver thread that was the canal which led out to Lake Erie. Soon he would be on another lake and off to a new home in a new state.

Tom's First Train Ride

"FATHER, look! There must be a fire ahead. See the smoke," cried Tom. He crawled over the crates and boxes to the front of the wagon, where Mr. Edison was sitting next to Sandy. "Oh, let's hurry, please, Father," Tom said, pulling at his right eyebrow, as he always did when he was excited.

Mr. Edison glanced at Sandy and winked. Then he turned around to Tom and said, "Son, that's just the smoke from the train you're going to ride on. There *is* a fire up ahead, but it's all in the firebox of the locomotive. Nobody's house is burning. No one is in danger."

Mrs. Edison pulled her shawl tighter and said to Mr. Edison, "No wonder people in Milan didn't want the railroad to come through their town. The women would have to do a washing every time the train passed through. I can just see the clotheslines with all that smoke blowing over the yards."

Tom paid no attention to his mother's remarks. He thought the billowing smoke was a fine sight, and he did his best to hurry Sandy and the horses on their way. "Where does the smoke come from, Father?"

"Wood is being burned in the firebox to make steam. Steam makes the locomotive go, and it pulls the coaches," Mr. Edison explained. "Now if you watch very closely, you will see the station of Norwalk, Ohio, as soon as we turn the bend in the road."

No one had to tell Tom to watch closely. He stepped over the various boxes and bundles and sat down again by Pitt. Pitt and Tannie were almost as excited as Tom, even though they had both seen a train before. None of the Edison family, however, had ever ridden on one.

Sandy pulled back on the reins a little and Tom felt the wagon go more slowly. They were going around the bend in the road. Tom scrambled to his feet and held onto Pitt's shoulder. He wanted to be sure to see everything that could be seen.

"There it is! There it is!" Tom shouted at the top of his voice. He pulled off his hat and, with the wind blowing his thatch of blond hair in his eyes, he waved it at the station. Then he waved to the big black locomotive that was standing on the track beside the little frame building.

"Hold on there, Tom," cried Pitt. He grabbed Tom's knees. "We'll soon stop this wagon and then you can jump. But don't do it yet!"

Just then Sandy guided the wagon up to the hitching posts behind the station. Tom had jumped to the ground and disappeared around the corner of the building long before Sandy climbed down.

"Better watch Tom, Mr. Edison," Sandy remarked, "or he'll be up in the engineer's cab asking a hundred questions before the engineer can guess what is happening to him."

"You look after Tom, Pitt. I'll see that your mother and Tannie find a place to sit in the station while I get the tickets," Mr. Edison said.

Pitt went off in the direction his brother had taken. When he came up to the tracks where the train was standing, he found Tom talking to a man who Pitt guessed at once was the engineer. He was tall and red faced, and his blue cap was pulled down almost over his eyes. He wore heavy gloves on his hands.

Pitt went up to the pair and said to the engineer, "Is my brother asking his usual number of questions, sir?"

58

"So this is your brother! Well, he has been here about three minutes, and I'd say he has asked ten questions already. But they are all good ones. Especially the last one was good."

"Pitt," Tom said, hurrying over to his brother's side, "I just asked Mr. Benjamin—that's the engineer—if I could ride with him to Detroit."

"You did? What did Mr. Benjamin say?"

"You came up just then, and he hasn't had a chance to answer. May I, Mr. Benjamin?" Tom asked, looking up anxiously into the engineer's eyes. "I won't ask any questions, I'll be as quiet as a mouse."

"I wouldn't take you a mile if you didn't ask questions," the engineer told Tom. He reached down and laid a hand on Tom's wind-blown hair. "But you will have to have your folks' permission before I can let you ride with me."

"Here comes my father now. Ask him! Ask him!" Tom pleaded.

"What does Tom want?" Mr. Edison asked as he drew closer to the little group.

"Father—" Tom pulled Mr. Edison over to him—"this is Mr. Benjamin, the engineer on the train. He says if I'll be sure to ask questions I may ride with him in the locomotive to Detroit. May I, Father? May I, please?"

"Why, Tom, the next thing we know you'll be wanting to help run the train, and then where would we be?" laughed his father.

Mr. Benjamin turned to Mr. Edison. "I'd be very glad to have Tom ride a few miles with me, if you and his mother wouldn't mind. He won't be any trouble, and I think he ought to know how a train is run."

"If his mother says he may, I have no objection. Ah, here is Mrs. Edison now. Nancy, Tom has already made a friend of the engineer. He has asked Tom to ride with him in the engine for a few miles. What do you say?"

"Is it safe?" asked Mrs. Edison.

"He'll be just as safe as you, ma'am."

"Well, Tom, if the engineer thinks you won't bother him too much, you may ride with him for a few miles. But don't touch anything and be careful, please."

Before Tom had a chance to say thank you, a man came out of the station calling, "All aboooooard! All aboooooard!" Tom had just time enough to tell Sandy good-by before the engineer lifted him high into the air and up into the locomotive cab. Mr. and Mrs. Edison and Tannie and Pitt were helped aboard one of the two coaches.

In the locomotive Mr. Benjamin began to explain the firebox to Tom.

"You remember seeing the thing on top that looks like a chimney? It's the smokestack, Tom. This box you see here has flues that run to the stack. It is called a 'firebox.' "

"What is that pipe coming out of the firebox?"

"That is one of the flues. The smoke goes through the flue and then out the smokestack," Mr. Benjamin told Tom.

"We pump water into this boiler by the firebox," he went on. "The fire in the box heats the water, just as a stove would. The water gets so hot that it boils."

"Then what happens?" Tom asked.

"Well," said Mr. Benjamin, "then we have steam."

"Where does the steam go?" asked Tom.

"It goes through one of these long tubes." Mr. Benjamin pointed to the tubes coming out of the boiler. "It goes through the tubes to cylinders. There is a cylinder on either side of the locomotive."

"What's a cylinder?"

"A cylinder looks about like a butter churn. It has a plunger which works back and forth in it. The plunger is called a piston rod. You see, steam is forced into the cylinder. It pushes the piston rod back and forth.

"The piston rods are attached to the two back drive wheels, and when they go back and forth they turn the wheels around."

Mr. Benjamin went on talking and working at the same time.

"When I press this lever," he said, pointing to a long handle attached to the tube which carried the steam, "it lets the steam out. When I push the lever up, the locomotive moves. When I push it down, the locomotive stops."

"Why?" asked Tom.

"Because, Tom, there is no steam in the cylinder when the lever is down."

The train was going very fast by this time. Tom asked Mr. Benjamin how fast it was going. The engineer told him it was going about fifteen miles an hour.

63

Then he took Tom's hand. "How would you like to run the train? Put your hand on this lever."

Tom put his fingers around the lever. It shook. Tom saw his hand shake, too.

"Why can't I hold my hand still?" he asked.

"Because of the vibration, Tom. The steam is so strong and it presses so hard that it vibrates, or shakes, everything it touches.

"How did you like running the train?" Mr. Benjamin asked as he took over the lever. The train was approaching a little town where it would stop to get water. It was time for Tom to go up into the coach with the rest of his family.

"It was fun. Thank you, Mr. Benjamin, for a wonderful trip." The train came to a standstill. The engineer helped Tom down from the locomotive. "Good-by, Mr. Benjamin! I hope I see you again sometime."

"Good-by, Tom," the engineer called. He

watched Tom until he saw the conductor help the little boy into the coach.

The conductor pushed open the door, and for the first time Tom saw the inside of a coach. He looked around for his mother and father. They were sitting together on a hard wooden bench. They could look across the aisle and watch the people on the other side.

Tom sat down between Tannie and Pitt. He began telling them all about the locomotive and what made a train go. He was so excited that he even forgot to notice Lulu in her box. She was on the seat beside Tannie.

The rest of the trip went so fast that it didn't seem at all as if a day had passed when the conductor came to the door and shouted:

"Next stop is Detroit! Get your baggage together. Next stop is Detroit!"

The House in
the Grove

"How MUCH farther is it, sir?" Tom asked, as the wagon bumped along the road.

"About three more miles," answered the driver of the wagon.

It was early morning, and the Edisons were on their way to the new home on the outskirts of Port Huron. The boat that carried them across Lake St. Clair had docked late the night before. Mr. Edison had carried sleepy Tom to the hotel and put him to bed with his brother Pitt. Tom had slept soundly until Pitt awakened him just before breakfast. And now they bumped along in the wagon on the dirt road which turned off from the main highway. Mr. Edison and Pitt had gone on ahead to open the house. They were to take one wagonload of furniture there before Mrs. Edison and Tannie and Tom arrived.

The road was very narrow. It was lined on each side by tall pine trees. Here and there Tom saw a house set far back among the trees. In some places the only sign that a house might be hidden by the trees was a fence or perhaps a lane leading from the road.

"What is that big building over there?" Tom asked.

"That's the schoolhouse," said the driver. "And a meaner teacher you'll never want to meet. Mr. Crawford is his name. Looks to me as if you might be old enough for that school, son," he added. He whipped the two horses to a faster trot.

"Will I have to go there, Mother?" Tom asked. He had a worried look on his face.

68

"Yes, I expect we had better send you this year, Tom." His mother smiled. "I doubt if Mr. Crawford is really as bad as he sounds. If you study your lessons every day, I am sure you'll get along well."

Then Mrs. Edison turned to the driver. "You see, we haven't sent Tom to school yet because he hasn't been very strong. We let him have plenty of fresh air and sunshine so that he would get stronger. But he is still small for his age. I was a teacher myself, and I have taught him at home. I'm sure that Tom will like the school."

"Maybe," was all the driver had time to say to Mrs. Edison's long speech. Ahead of them Mr. Edison was standing in a lane.

As the wagon slowed down, Tom jumped to the road and ran up to his father. "Quick, Father, let me see the house," he cried.

"If you look straight up the lane you'll be able to see it," Mr. Edison told his son. And there it was—a large white frame house almost surrounded by a thick grove of trees. A long porch ran across the front.

"It's so big, Samuel," said Mrs. Edison as she came up to Tom and his father. The Edisons stood and gazed at the house for a few moments.

"Now where is Tom?" exclaimed his mother, looking around for him.

"I guess he ran up the lane, Nancy. You go on to the house. I want to talk to the driver about the rest of the luggage," Mr. Edison said.

The two women walked up the lane. Tannie was patiently carrying Lulu in her box. Once again Tom had forgotten all about her.

"The trees are so pretty, Mother," Tannie remarked.

Most of the trees were pine, but there were a few tall, very full trees with broad leaves. They were maple trees. There were also oak trees. The oaks would be lovely in the fall and winter. Their leaves would stay a long time and would be a beautiful shade of red most of the year.

When they came up to the house, they could see better how beautiful it was. Tom and Pitt were standing on the front steps and Tom was excitedly calling, "Hurry, Mother! Hurry! I've been all through the house already. There's a wide hall so big that we can play games in it. And all the ceilings are twice as tall as Father."

Mrs. Edison and Tannie followed Tom through the house. Each of the rooms had long windows which looked out on the woods and the St. Clair River. Each had a wide fireplace, too.

Mrs. Edison hurried on to the kitchen, which was another large room with many windows and a fireplace. There was a wood-burning stove for cooking.

Upstairs, Tom told her, were six bedrooms. It was a large house for four people.

"It's so big, Tannie, that I wish you didn't have to hurry back to your own new home in Milan," Mrs. Edison said. "We will rattle around in it like dried apples in a barrel."

By this time Mr. Edison had brought in the rest of their belongings and sent the driver back to Port Huron. The house had already been cleaned by some of the neighbors, so the family could begin the work of moving in.

First of all Mrs. Edison made everyone put on old clothes. Then she had Tom and Pitt bring in the clean, fresh straw which was stacked on the back porch. This was to cover all the downstairs floors. She made the boys spread it so thickly that not a single floor board showed. This would keep out any cold air from under the house.

"Now be sure you don't leave any humps, Tom," called Mrs. Edison. She stood in the doorway of the kitchen watching him. Tom and Pitt

were laying the straw on the parlor floor. They were working very carefully.

It seemed to Tom that he had been working with the straw for a long, long time before his mother was finally satisfied. Then she had Mr. Edison and Pitt bring in the rolled-up carpeting.

It was a very pretty rose-colored carpeting with large flowers in it. Very carefully the boys laid it in strips over the straw, and then Mr. Edison stretched it tight and tacked it to the floor. Soon the entire downstairs was completely covered, and the rooms were ready for the furniture. Mrs. Edison let Tom unpack the family keepsakes and put them on the walnut whatnot.

"I think I ought not go to school until next week," said Tom. "I can't leave with all the work to do here. Can I, Father?"

"Tom's right, Father," said Tannie, with a wink in Tom's direction. "You'll need him to help."

74

"Maybe you two are right," Mr. Edison said, as he looked at the many boxes. "But on Monday, school it is!"

Then Tom went out to the barn to show Lulu her new home. She waddled around and looked in every corner. Finally she settled in the new nest Tom had fixed for her, quite satisfied.

Tom ran back to the house. "I'm getting very hungry," he announced as he walked into the kitchen. Tannie was there, busily sewing new curtains for the long windows.

A fire was burning in the fireplace, and Tom warmed his hands. In early March it was much colder in Michigan than it had been in Ohio.

Mr. Edison came into the kitchen, looking at his big watch. "My goodness," he said, "here it is almost three o'clock, and we haven't had a bite to eat since early this morning at the hotel! I think we should all stop and help Mother get supper."

After supper Tom said, "Are we going to name our new house? Many people have names for their homes. I think we should, too."

"That's a good idea, Tom. The house and this beautiful grove of trees around it should have a special name."

Tom shut his eyes and thought. "I know, Mother! Let's call it the House in the Grove."

"Oh, fine, Tom! I like the sound of that." Tannie smiled.

Everyone else liked it, too, and agreed that there couldn't be a better name for the new house.

Mr. Edison went over to the fireplace. "Today was the day for the packet boat to come. It comes three days a week. I wonder if we got any mail."

"You can see when you take me into town tomorrow," Tannie said.

"Oh, Tannie, it has been grand having you to

76

help. I wish you didn't have to leave," said her mother.

"Please stay, Tannie," Tom begged. "Can't you stay? We have plenty of room."

"How well I know that!" laughed Tannie. "But no, Tom. I must go back to Milan and get ready to move into *my* new house."

"You will come often to see us, won't you, Tannie?" said Pitt.

"I'll come here and you can come to see me. Why, soon there will be railroads all over this country, and it will be nothing to take a train and go visiting."

The next afternoon Mr. Edison took Tannie to the Port Huron station. When he came back he brought a copy of the Detroit *Free Press*, one of the best newspapers in the country.

The family sat around the kitchen table while Mr. Edison read aloud the headlines of the paper. They were about an American naval officer named Commodore Matthew Perry, who was in command of a large fleet of ships.

In 1852 the President of the United States, Millard Fillmore, had sent Commodore Perry to Japan with his many ships.

The United States wanted to have an American harbor in Japan. They wanted to trade with the Japanese people. Commodore Perry had delivered an important message from President Fillmore to the Japanese. Then he went on to China.

Now, in 1854, Commodore Perry was back in Japan, in the city of Yokohama, the newspaper said. The people of Japan were almost ready to sign a treaty with the United States. They were going to let the Americans have two ports.

"Why do we want to trade with Japan?" Tom asked, when Mr. Edison finished reading the newspaper.

"That is the way countries make money, Tom.

We want to be friendly with all nations and all kinds of people."

It was to become a habit of the Edisons to sit at the round kitchen table after dinner. They listened to Mr. Edison read from the newspaper. That way Tom learned many things about current events and the history of his own country. He remembered them all.

First Day
at School

"WILL YOU walk as far as the school with us, Pitt?" Tom begged as he put his coat on. It was Monday morning and that meant school.

"Since it's your first day, Tom, I will. But after this you will have to go by yourself. Why don't you like the idea of going to school?" Pitt asked.

Before Tom could answer, Mrs. Edison joined them on the front porch, and they set off. The schoolhouse was about half a mile up the road. Tom remembered how drab the building looked.

He had not seen the teacher, but he had heard the boys and girls talk about him as they passed the Edison lane on the way home from school. The children laughed and shouted as they ran down the road. Tom had heard several of them say, "I don't like Mr. Crawford. He isn't fair."

One day a boy had said, "Mr. Crawford won't ever let us ask any questions except about the lessons. He's too strict."

Tom was sure that he wasn't going to like school.

He was in no hurry to get there, but Mrs. Edison and Pitt walked fast along the road. Tom carried his new green lunch box and slate under his arm. He had also the pad of sketching paper and colored pencils Pitt had given him for his birthday. He was very proud of them. He had already made many sketches. His favorite was a picture of Lulu sitting on her eggs. He wished now that he could stay at home and draw the House in the Grove.

"Why are you in such a hurry, Pitt?" he asked.

as he skipped a step or two to keep up with his brother.

"I have work to do, Tom. I'm going to see about a job at the livery stable in town. I have to be on time."

"Here we are, Tom," said Mrs. Edison. They had come to the schoolyard. It was almost eight o'clock. The children had stopped playing games and were picking up their books and slates.

"Good-by, Tom" said Pitt. "Don't worry about school. You are going to like it." He went hurrying on toward town. Mrs. Edison went ahead into the schoolhouse.

The children all stared at Tom. They were curious about the new pupil from Ohio. They saw a very short boy, with a body so small that his head looked almost too large for it. His thick blond hair was falling over his eyes, which were a bright gray.

Tom was interested in everything. He was happy to see all the children. He had never had many friends his own age.

Before he had time to get acquainted, his mother called to him from the door. Tom went over to join her. Only one room of the house was used for the schoolroom. In the center was a stove. Beside it were two black buckets full of wood. At one end of the room was a large stone fireplace. It didn't look as if it were used often. It was clean and free from smoke.

"Tom," said his mother, "this is Mr. Crawford, your teacher."

Tom looked up. Mr. Crawford was a very tall man. He had thick dark hair. Over pale-blue eyes were the heaviest black eyebrows Tom had ever seen.

Mr. Crawford did not smile. "Your mother tells me you have had no schooling," he said. "You will begin at the first grade."

"But I am seven, Mr. Crawford," said Tom.

"One of the first things we learn in this school, Thomas Alva, is not to talk back to our teacher. You will do well to remember that.

"Here is your seat," he told Tom. He walked over to the row of benches and desks by the fireplace and pointed.

"This will be nice. It is right by the fireplace," said Tom, feeling a little better.

"There is never a fire in that fireplace. The wood stove in the center of the room gives enough heat. An open fire would take the students' attention from their lessons."

Mrs. Edison was talking to one of the boys who had come in. School was about to begin.

"You may go now, Mrs. Edison," Mr. Crawford said. "I will see that Thomas Alva brings the necessary materials home to study. We require that each pupil study at home every night. Good morning, Mrs. Edison." Mr. Crawford showed Tom's mother to the door, then he started toward the front of the room.

Tom suddenly felt very much alone in the big schoolroom. He hadn't even been able to tell his mother good-by. All the children were still staring at him.

Mr. Crawford stood at the front of the room and rapped on his desk with a long rod.

"School has begun. You will all keep your faces to the front. The new pupil is Thomas Alva Edison. He will be in the first grade until he proves himself. If he does good work he will be put in the second grade where he belongs."

Tom's first class was reading, and he had no trouble with that. He always read at home. Sometimes he read the newspaper his father brought. He could figure out many words in the big black headlines. When he came to a word he didn't know, he would spell it out. Someone would tell him what it meant.

The next class was penmanship.

"The pupils will all take their slates."

The lesson began. The children did what Mr. Crawford told them to do. That is, all the children but Tom. He was holding his sketch pad on his slate and was drawing a picture of the new House in the Grove.

He could hear Mr. Crawford in the distance. "Round and round and round. Crayon up!" But Tom paid no attention.

"I said 'Crayon up,' Thomas Alva."

Still Tom did not hear. He was too busy at his drawing.

Suddenly he noticed that it was very quiet in the big room. He could feel Mr. Crawford coming toward him. Then the teacher was looking over Tom's shoulder. He snatched the paper out of Tom's hands.

"Thomas Alva Edison! Is this an example of penmanship?"

86

"I—no—that—no, sir. No, Mr. Crawford. This is our new house, sir," said Tom. He was frightened and wished now he had paid attention to Mr. Crawford. The teacher looked cross. In fact, he was so cross that his eyebrows were going up and down. "His eyebrows move when he's angry," Tom thought.

"Thomas Alva, you will take that paper and the colored pencils home this afternoon. *Never* bring them back again. Now, go and sit in that corner until lunchtime."

Tom went over to the corner. He sat down on the low round stool. He kept so quiet that soon the children forgot he was there. Tom began to feel hungry. He remembered all the good things his mother had put in his lunch box. The lessons went on and on. Then a sharp rap on the desk made him jump.

Mr. Crawford was standing up.

"You will put your books away and walk

quietly to the side yard. It is lunchtime. And no talking on the way out, mind you!"

Tom got up and started toward his lunch box.

"Thomas Alva, come to my desk," Mr. Crawford called.

Tom walked over to the teacher's desk. He looked up at Mr. Crawford's eyebrows. They were not going up and down anymore. Maybe he wasn't angry any longer.

"I expect the strictest attention from all my pupils. You have come here to learn to read and write and do arithmetic. You cannot learn these things by drawing pictures. I have no interest in drawing." He picked up Tom's picture and tore it across. "From now on, Thomas Alva, you will listen to me carefully and do exactly as I tell you. Is that clear?"

"Yes, Mr. Crawford."

"You may have your lunch."

Tom went slowly back to his bench. He reached for his box. It wasn't there! He looked under the bench. He looked under the lid of the desk. His good lunch was nowhere to be seen. And it had a big piece of gingerbread in it. Tom felt hungrier every minute.

He went out into the yard. Under a tree a group of boys were sitting, eating, and laughing.

"Have you seen a green lunch box?" Tom asked them.

"I saw Michael Oates with a green box," said a redheaded boy. "He's the boy over there in a dark blue shirt. He's in the fourth grade."

Tom walked over to the tall blond boy.

"Are you Michael Oates?" he asked.

"Yes. Why?" said Michael.

Tom pointed to the boy with the red hair. "He said you have my lunch box."

Michael looked surprised for a minute. Then he laughed a deep rolling laugh.

"I wasn't going to tell you, so you'd have to hunt for it, but here it is. This has been a pretty bad morning for you. You don't deserve any more teasing. Old 'Crawfish' has it in for you. He'll get over it. But it doesn't pay to talk back to him."

90

Then Michael gave Tom his lunch box. "Sit down, Tom, and eat with me and my friend James Clancy."

"Say," said James, "where is that picture, Tom?"

Tom told him that Mr. Crawford had torn it up.

"I wish I could draw," said Michael. "I could think up a good picture of Mr. Crawford. I would make him sit on that stool over in the corner. His knees would almost reach to his chin."

The boys all laughed and laughed. They could just see Mr. Crawford sitting in the corner on the little low stool where Tom had spent the morning.

By the time the big bell rang for afternoon classes, Tom had decided that school might not be too bad. Especially at lunchtime.

The Basement Laboratory

MARCH AND April went by slowly for Tom. He was very unhappy at school. He had made a lot of friends, but Mr. Crawford was not one of them. The teacher never liked the kind of questions Tom asked. Poor Tom spent many mornings sitting on the low stool in the corner.

One day in May Tom came rushing into the house with all his books in his arms. His cap was pulled low over his gray eyes.

"Mother! Mother! I'm never going back to that school again!"

Mrs. Edison came hurrying from the kitchen. She met Tom in the hall. "Why, Tom, what is the matter? Why aren't you going back? Did something go wrong?"

"Mr. Crawford says I'm 'addled.' Mother, what does 'addled' mean?"

"It means you don't think clearly, Tom," his mother said. "But I know you do."

"We were having a reading lesson," Tom explained. "It was all about a river in Ohio. It ran up a hill. The Huron River didn't do that. I asked Mr. Crawford how water could run uphill. He slammed his book shut. He pounded his desk with his fist. Then he came over to me with his eyebrows going up and down and up and down. He said, 'Thomas Alva, you always ask entirely too many questions. You are addled.'"

"We will not have you in that school any longer, Tom," said Mrs. Edison. "You have every right to ask questions. If Mr. Crawford were a good teacher he would be glad that you are interested and curious. This is how people learn. You must never stop asking questions. Keep asking until a problem is clear in your own mind."

"How can I learn things, Mother, if I don't go to school?"

"I'll teach you here at home. When it is nice weather we'll have our lessons out on the front porch. Until then we'll have them in here by the stove. We will have fun learning."

"But do you know all about arithmetic, Mother?" Tom asked.

Mrs. Edison laughed. "I know enough, Tom. We'll do problems in arithmetic. We will read from all the books in the parlor. We will learn about the history of our country and about the history of countries across the sea. Yes, Tom, you can learn many things right here at home."

The next day Mrs. Edison went to see Mr. Crawford. She told him that Tom would no longer come to his school. He wanted to know if Tom always asked such foolish questions.

Mrs. Edison told him exactly what she had told Tom. She said he should be glad when his pupils asked questions. That was the best way for children to learn.

Tom really enjoyed his lessons at home. When the days began to be warmer, they had their school on the front porch. As the other children passed the Edison home, they wished that they, too, might have Mrs. Edison as a teacher. She and Tom always seemed to be having a good time. They would laugh as they studied.

One of the boys often came up the lane to the House in the Grove. He was Michael Oates, the boy who had hidden Tom's lunch box. Michael was working now for the Edisons after school and on Saturday.

He did many little chores around the house and farm. He took care of the three cows and the chickens and geese. It was his duty to keep the barn clean. He helped Mr. Edison plow the garden plot for summer vegetables. Sometimes Tom would help Michael. The two boys had become very good friends, even though Michael was ten years old and Tom was only seven.

Most of the time, though, Tom was too busy to help Michael. He had become interested in

knowing what everything was made of. He studied all sorts of objects and tried to find how they were made. He would look at the water in a glass and try to imagine how it could be made of gases. His mother had told him that it was.

She said that Tom was studying a science called chemistry when he tried to find what substances things were made of or how to combine substances so that they made new things.

Tom had been reading a book by a man named Richard Parker. He had written about all sorts of experiments in chemistry. Mr. Parker had a room called a laboratory, in which he tried to make many different things. He had many bottles on the shelves in this room. The bottles held substances called chemicals. Some were liquid and some were solid. Tom learned that by mixing certain chemicals together he could make new, different ones. He thought he would like to have a laboratory like Mr. Parker's.

Under the House in the Grove was a large cellar. In part of this basement the Edisons kept barrels of apples and potatoes. Mrs. Edison planned to put all the food she canned down there. But that still left a big space.

In one corner was a rickety table with shelves over it. Mr. Edison said Tom could use that part of the basement for his workshop.

One day when Michael had finished his chores, he and Tom went all over town looking for bottles. They found big ones and small ones. They got blue ones and green ones and even some pretty red ones.

Tom and Michael found thirty bottles. When they came home Tom took his sketching pad and cut out thirty little squares of paper. Then he took his red pencil. He drew a picture of a skull on each square. Underneath that he drew pictures of crossbones. Over the pictures he put the word POISON.

Then Tom and Michael went into the kitchen. Out of the flour bin they took some flour. They put it in a pan, and Tom added water. There was already a fire in the big cookstove. Mrs. Edison had started dinner, Tom discovered. There was a pan of potatoes cooking. But this was much more important. Tom moved the potatoes over and put his flour and water on to cook.

As the mixture got hot Tom stirred and stirred until there were no lumps left in it. When it came to a boil he took his pan off the stove. He let it cool. When it was cool enough that it wouldn't burn his fingers, he and Michael went down into the basement with the paste.

Tom put some of this mixture on the back of each of the little squares of paper that said POISON. Then he pasted them to the bottles. Mr. Parker had marked some of his bottles with that word. My, but they looked nice! Thirty bright, clean bottles lined up on the two shelves. Tom and Michael stepped back to admire their work.

"Now let's go outside and see what we can find, Michael," said Tom.

The two boys hurried out into the yard to hunt for things to put in their bottles. They got feathers from the chicken yard. They went to the barn and found pieces of dried cornstalks. From the center of these they took the pith. Then they gathered dried corn.

From the kitchen they took sugar. In the cupboard by the pump was cotton. Tom put all these things in separate bottles. They would do until the boys could buy real chemicals.

That was the beginning of Tom Edison's first laboratory. It was a bad beginning, Mrs. Edison thought. When she went into the kitchen to finish dinner, the potatoes weren't cooking. Tom had forgotten to put them back on the fire when the paste was finished.

Tom Tries
an Experiment

"How MANY more loads do you think we need, Michael?" Tom asked as he stumbled along after his friend. He was carrying a bushel basket full of apples. "How many, Michael?"

"That one will do it, Tom." Michael was loading the baskets of apples into the wagon. Roman, the horse, was pawing at the ground. He wanted to start.

Tom and Michael had been working all summer in the garden and the orchard. Mr. Edison had given them a plot of ground to work. They raised their own vegetables and sold them to people in town. Business had been good.

Mr. Edison had bought them the wagon. He had told the boys he would let them pick out a horse. Tom and Michael had searched all over Port Huron. Finally they had found Roman. He was a bay horse. He was long and had what Michael called a "dip" in his back. That was really what gave him his name.

Tom and his mother had been studying Roman history. Mrs. Edison had read aloud to Tom from a book called *The Decline and Fall of the Roman Empire*. As soon as Tom rode behind the horse, he told Michael that his name ought to be Roman.

"But why call him that, Tom?" Michael asked.

"Look at his back," Tom said, with a laugh. "See how it rises and falls when he walks? Just like the Roman Empire."

That had been enough history for Michael. He was satisfied to let Tom do all the learning. He believed everything Tom told him. He had thought they couldn't make any money from the truck garden. But Tom convinced him they could make more money that way than by doing odd jobs around the town.

Now it was September and the boys had their last wagonload of apples. They had sold fruit, potatoes, baskets of apples, and every kind of vegetable all summer.

Tom and Michael would drive into town. They would tie the wagon at the hitching post in front of the general store, where there was a trough of water for Roman. The two boys would take a basket and go from door to door selling their produce. But sometimes they didn't even get into town. Women in the houses along the road might buy all their wares.

This particular day that was just what happened. By the time Tom and Michael got into Port Huron they had only three apples left. They ate these as they drove up to the hitching post.

"What are we going to do, Tom?" Michael asked as he munched his apple.

"I'm going to the chemist's shop. I want to buy some mercury."

"What is mercury?" asked Michael.

"Well," said Tom, "mercury looks like silver. You can put a drop of it on the table and it will roll. It looks like a little silver ball."

"What will you do with it, Tom?"

"I am going to make a thermometer," Tom told him proudly.

"Well, I guess maybe you can do it, but I never could," said Michael as they jumped down from the wagon.

The boys walked toward the chemist's shop. Tom loved to visit Mr. Stevensen's shop. He thought it surely must have a million different bottles. Each one had some kind of chemical in it. Some of the chemicals were of beautiful colors.

105

Tom had been saving his money each week. Every Saturday he had bought something for his laboratory, but he continued to save most of his earnings. Last week he had bought sulphur. It was a bright yellow powder. He had burned some and it had made a blue flame. It had made a suffocating gas, too. Tom had had to hurry out of his laboratory to get his breath.

This was the last trip to the chemist. He would now have all thirty bottles full. Mr. Stevensen had taught Tom to write the names of the chemicals to go on his bottles. When he put on the real name he took off the word POISON.

Even on a bottle of water he had a label which said H_2O. Tom knew that meant water was made of two things. It had two parts of hydrogen and one part of oxygen.

The boys went into the store. "Hello, Tom. Hello, Michael," Mr. Stevensen said. "What will it be today?"

"I would like to have some mercury, Mr. Stevensen."

"That is pretty expensive, Tom."

"I have almost one hundred dollars," Tom said.

The chemist whistled. "Where did you get that much money?"

"Michael and I have each saved that much from our truck garden," Tom explained.

"That's right, Mr. Stevensen," said Michael. "We each will have about one hundred dollars when we count up what we made today and add it to what we made all summer."

"You boys are certainly energetic," Mr. Stevensen said. He reached for the big blue bottle of mercury. "I was telling a man just this morning about you and Tom. I said that no one would ever catch you two napping. Here's your mercury, Tom. That will be two dollars."

Tom paid for it and took the bottle, and he and Michael left the shop. They unhitched Roman and started home.

"Michael," said Tom, "I wonder how birds fly. It looks easy."

"If we had wings I guess we could fly, too," Michael said, as he watched a crow fly off into the distance.

"Well, there must be other ways to fly," Tom said. He pulled on his right eyebrow. "I have some Seidlitz powders in the laboratory."

"Whatever are they, Tom?"

108

"When you mix a blue powder with a white one in water a gas forms," Tom told him. "Now gas is lighter than air. If you——"

"Not *I*, Tom. No, sirree. I'm not going to drink anything chemical," said Michael, looking scared.

"Wait until I explain to you, Michael. If you were to drink it, your stomach would fill up with gas. Yes, and then you would float up in the air. We'll try it," he finished. Then he called to Roman, "Gidup, Roman. We want to get home in a hurry."

Michael didn't say a word all the way home. Tom didn't notice because he was busy thinking about Michael flying.

They drove up the lane of the House in the Grove. They put Roman in the barn and gave him his oats bag. Then Tom called to Michael, who was hanging up the harness, "Come on down to the laboratory when you are through."

Tom ran on ahead, down the outside stairs to the basement. He went over to his table. He reached above the table to his shelves. There were two bottles marked SEIDLITZ POWDER. Tom took them down and put one dose of each powder into separate glasses. He called, "Hurry up, Michael. Hurry up!"

Michael came slowly into the laboratory. He didn't look very happy.

"Now, Michael, think how wonderful it will be to fly over the St. Clair River. You can almost see Detroit, you'll be so high. Our house will look like a doll's house."

"I don't want to see Detroit," said Michael.

"We'll be famous for this experiment, Michael," said Tom. "All you have to do is drink this. Now let's go out into the yard."

Tom ran out of the basement. Michael followed more slowly.

He found Tom standing by the barn. He held

a glass in each hand. "Come over here, Michael. It won't hurt. I promise you."

"How do you know?" Michael asked. But he reached for the glass. He was convinced by this time that Tom knew what he was doing.

Tom poured the contents of one glass into the other. It quickly foamed up. "Drink it! Drink it fast!" Tom cried.

Michael took it all in one gulp.

"Now fly, Michael! Fly!" yelled Tom excitedly. "Wave your arms!"

Michael's eyes got big and bright. He moved his arms up and down. Then, suddenly, he moved them over his stomach.

"How do you feel?" cried Tom. "Can you fly?"

"I—I—feel funny," said Michael. He ran into the house.

Michael was sick. He didn't fly.

Tom went slowly back to the basement. He had just put the bottles of Seidlitz powder back on the shelf when he heard his mother.

"Thomas Alva Edison! Come here."

He knew she was very angry. She never called him all three names unless she was. Tom ran up the stairs. This was no time to walk.

Mrs. Edison was standing by the back door. "Why did you make Michael take that drink? You knew it couldn't make him fly."

112

"But it made a gas in his stomach, Mother. Gas is lighter than air. He *should* have flown," said Tom, a little meek by this time.

"Michael is sick in bed. That was a terrible thing to do," said Mrs. Edison. "I am afraid that you must go to bed without your supper. And another thing, you will have to destroy all your bottles in the laboratory."

"Oh, Mother, not that! Please. I won't do it again. I promise," begged Tom. He was almost in tears. He had spent so much time collecting those bottles. He had spent his vegetable money buying chemicals. He couldn't just throw them all away!

"I'm afraid that is the only thing to do, Tom," his mother said sternly.

"Couldn't I put a lock on the door and just go in sometimes?" asked Tom hopefully.

Mrs. Edison stood a long time thinking. Tom had learned a great many things from his laboratory. Michael was not too sick. If Tom could learn that he must never experiment on people again, maybe he would not have to give up his workshop.

"If your father can put a lock on the door, then you may keep your chemicals. But, Tom, you must *never* ask anyone to drink any of them again. Is that clear?"

"Yes, Mother," Tom answered. Going to bed without his supper wouldn't be nearly so bad, now that he could keep his laboratory.

Tom's First Telegraph

It was four years since the Edisons had moved to the House in the Grove. Tom and his mother had spent many hours studying and reading. Tom knew he was lucky to have a good mother to help him learn at home.

Tom's father had spent the fall of 1854 building a tower at the end of their garden. It was made of wood. It was one hundred feet high, and there were wooden steps which went clear up to the top. On top of the tower was a platform. Tom could stand up there and see up the St. Clair River. On clear days he could see as far as Lake Huron.

Mr. Edison charged people twenty-five cents to climb to the top of the tower to see the countryside. At first almost nobody came. Then the men who owned the railroad began to put up signs in their trains. The signs told the passengers what beautiful things they could see from the tower.

Across the road from the Edisons' house was Fort Gratiot. It was on the St. Clair River. The fort had been built in 1686 by French soldiers. They were afraid of the Indians and wanted protection. Later, when the French and the Indians were at war, the French soldiers used this fort to defend themselves.

But in 1854, when Mr. Edison built his wooden tower, there were no soldiers at Fort Gratiot. Everyone thought there would be no more wars in that part of the country.

The fort was in a big woods that went right down to the banks of the St. Clair River. It was a fine place for picnics. When many people came to Fort Gratiot from Port Huron, Tom's father began to make money. Everyone wanted to climb to the top of the tower. Then they would have their picnics on the grounds of Fort Gratiot.

Now, in 1859, the old fort was again full of soldiers. But this time they were American soldiers. They had been sent there because there was talk that a civil war might come in the United States. If it did, people in the North wanted to have a fort and soldiers for protection.

Tom and his mother loved to sit on the platform on top of the tower when there was nobody around to bother them. Here they read about Columbus. Tom would stand by the railing and pretend he was Columbus. The platform made a fine ship. He would put his hands above his eyes and look at the river. He made believe that the St. Clair River was the great Atlantic

Ocean. Then he would look across it and shout to his mother, "Land! Land!"

He had discovered America.

Sometimes Tom would pretend he was Commodore Perry, sailing into the harbor at Yokohama with a message for the Emperor of Japan. It was fun, and at the same time Tom learned much about geography and history.

118

Tom's special friend now, besides Michael Oates, was James Clancy. He lived up the road. He and Tom were both twelve now.

Sometimes James wanted to tell Tom something right away, but he was too far off to run down to see him. He and Tom wished they had a way to send messages quickly. They had heard there was a new invention for this, called a telegraph. A man at one end of a wire could tap a metal key on an instrument called a sender. His messages would travel over the wire to a receiver at the other end.

Every night, as Mr. Edison read aloud from the newspaper, Tom thought about the telegraph. His father had told him that all the papers got their news over a telegraph wire.

If big newspapers could get news from all over the world on a telegraph, then surely Tom and James could have a telegraph wire between their houses.

The two boys spent many afternoons working on this idea. They got a great length of wire from the tinsmith at Port Huron. It would reach all the way from Tom's house to James's house. Then they collected lots of old bottles.

Finally they began to make their own telegraph system. They carefully broke the necks off the bottles. Then they drove nails through the necks of the bottles into trees and into fence posts along the road. Around the bottles they wound the wire. Then they made a sender and receiver for each end, and attached them to the wire.

While the boys were working, Tabby the house cat rubbed against Tom's legs. She gave Tom one of his ideas.

"Why, James, we won't need batteries for our telegraph wire. We can use Tabby!" said Tom excitedly, as he grabbed the cat.

"What do you mean, Tom?" asked James.

120

"Watch." Tom put Tabby on the table. She didn't like it very well. Tom put the very tip of her tail, where there were only long hairs, around the copper key and under the wire.

"You see, James, if we can get enough sparks of electricity from Tabby's fur, we won't have to spend our money on batteries. You help me rub her. Rub her fur hard the wrong way." Tom began to rub Tabby's back.

Then came such a howling and scratching from Tabby as Tom and James had never heard before. With one great lunge, she pulled her tail from under the wire and ran away.

"It was a good idea, James, but Tabby just didn't seem to like it, did she?" laughed Tom. "I guess we will have to get batteries and two sets of earphones, after all."

After the boys got the batteries and attached them to their telegraph system, they were ready to send their first message.

Tom and James had studied the Morse code. It had been invented by a man named Samuel Morse to send messages by telegraph. The code was really an alphabet in sounds. Each letter was a different combination of dots and dashes. The person sending the message spelled out words by taps. He held the key down a short time for a dot, longer for a dash. The person who received the message wrote the letters down as dots or dashes. "A" was · — "B" was — · · · Tom and James were both eager to try it.

James ran home. Tom was to give him time to get there and then send the first message.

Finally James sat at his end of the wire. He heard short and long noises. He was so excited that he could hardly wait for Tom's message. When James had written it down, he had:

· · · · · — — · ·

The message Tom had sent said "Hello."

Tom and James had invented their own tele-

graph system. From then on the boys sent messages all the time. Tom's father liked to stand by him and watch.

Tom taught his father how to work the key. One night Mr. Edison sent a message to James. It said, "Guess who?"

James sent a message back which said, "Mr. Edison." He knew it wasn't Tom. Mr. Edison had gone too slowly!

A Job on a Train

THE SUMMER of 1859 passed very quickly. Tom and his mother still had their lessons every day. But they no longer studied on the platform of the tower. Mr. Edison had had to tear it down. It was getting shaky and too dangerous to climb.

Pitt lived in Port Huron now. He had a good job working for the livery stable. He was so busy that he couldn't come home more often than once a month.

One night Mr. Edison came hurrying into the kitchen. Tom was helping his mother get dinner.

"I have just heard great news," Mr. Edison said, as he sat down.

"What kind of news, Father?" Tom asked.

"Well, son, it means progress for our town. The Grand Trunk Railway has finally been finished. We can now ride from Port Huron clear to Detroit."

The new railway had its beginning in Canada. The tracks ran right down to the St. Clair River. They stopped at a point across from the Edison farm at Fort Gratiot. During the last few months Tom had watched gangs of men laying the railroad tracks on the Michigan side of the river. The men had worked hard. Finally a train would run on that track to Port Huron.

"I just can't understand, Samuel," said Mrs. Edison, "how trains will get across the St. Clair River. They can't run on water."

"They will put the trains on the ferryboat," Tom explained.

"But, Tom, how can they do that?" his mother asked. "The trains must run on tracks."

126

"They will have tracks built right on the deck of the ferry. They will run the ferry into the slip on the Canadian side. The engineer will see that the tracks of the ferry fit those on the ground. Then he can run right onto the ferry," Tom finished.

"This is a busy world we live in," said Tom's mother, as she put the food on the table. "Come, supper is ready."

After supper Mr. Edison got the Detroit *Free Press* out of his pocket. He gave the paper to Tom.

"You read it to us, Tom. I think you'll be interested in what you see there on the front page."

Tom began reading aloud to his mother and father. The story in the newspaper was about the great celebration which was to be held the next day in Port Huron. The celebration was for the new railroad. It would be the first train to

127

come from Canadian shores. It would come across the St. Clair River on the ferryboat at Fort Gratiot and go on to Port Huron and Detroit.

There were to be a big new engine and three new, brightly painted coaches. A large group of Port Huron's citizens was to have the first ride in the new coaches. All the people around Port Huron were invited to come into town to watch the first trip the train was to take.

It wouldn't be a long trip that day, but the next trip would be all the way to Detroit.

"Oh, Father," cried Tom, "may we go, please? May we all go, please?"

"What do you think, Nancy?" Mr. Edison asked. He winked at Tom's mother.

"I think we should all go," she said. "But we'll have to go to bed early tonight so that we will be ready to get up early in the morning."

It was a sunny, cold day in November when

128

the Edisons started out for Port Huron the next morning. The roads were crowded. Everyone was going into town to see the new railroad. Everyone was dressed up in his best clothes. All were laughing and singing as the wagons passed on the road. Tom was so excited that he forgot his hat. His hair blew in the breeze. His gray eyes were big and bright.

At Port Huron there were so many people around the railroad station that Tom could not even see the tracks. He was still short, even though he was twelve now. He pushed his way through the crowds. As usual, he got away from his mother and father in his excitement and curiosity.

There on the tracks was the most beautiful sight Tom had ever seen. It was a big wood-burning locomotive. Its wheels were painted a bright red. All around the locomotive was a bright band of brass.

Behind the locomotive were three wooden coaches. They were painted a bright yellow. On the sides of the coaches were beautiful pictures. On the first coach was painted Niagara Falls. Mountains were painted on the second coach and a lake on the last one.

Tom was so thrilled that he could hardly stand still. He looked up into the face of a big man next to him. "Isn't it beautiful?" he said.

"It surely is, son," the man agreed. He was very tall, and he was smoking the biggest pipe Tom had ever seen.

"The smokestack looks exactly like a tall silk hat," Tom remarked.

"It does at that," the man said. "And look at the cowcatcher. That looks like some of these women's hoop skirts."

They both laughed at the picture the locomotive made.

"I wonder if——" Tom stopped. He saw the big man with the pipe turn to a friend who had just come up. He was saying, "We're going to need a boy to sell newspapers and candy on this train between Port Huron and Detroit."

Tom pricked up his ears. The man to whom he had been talking must have something to do with this railroad. Tom thought fast. He needed more equipment for his laboratory. Why couldn't he have that job and make money to buy more chemicals?

Tom turned to the big man with the pipe. "How would I do, sir?" he asked.

The man looked down at Tom. "You're mighty little. How old are you?"

"I'm twelve, sir. But I'll be thirteen in February, and this is November. I'm little but I'm strong, and I can do a lot of work."

The two men talked it over between themselves for a minute. The second man turned to Tom. "Where are your folks?"

"I'll go get them, sir. They are right here in this crowd."

He looked around and saw his father's head above most of the people around him.

"Father! Father! Come quick!" Tom called.

Tom's father and mother came hurrying over.

"Tom," said his mother, "you can get away from us faster than this train can get away from Port Huron. I *do* wish you would tell us before you go running off."

Tom was too busy to listen closely to his mother. He told his parents about his plan to

132

work on the new train. The two men talked to Mr. and Mrs. Edison. Finally they decided that Tom could take the job. He was getting to the age where he needed real work to do. He spent most of his time in his laboratory. Mrs. Edison thought he should be out in the air more. This would be a good chance to get him out of the basement.

Tom told the men that he would be at the station the next morning at six-thirty. The train would leave for Detroit at seven.

Then the Edisons watched the locomotive. Smoke was coming out of its "tall silk hat." It made a chugging noise. Finally it started up the new tracks. It was making its first real trip.

Men threw their hats into the air. They whistled and shouted. It was a great day. The Grand Trunk Railway had come to Port Huron, and Tom's first real job was on that same train.

The Underground Railway

It was the spring of 1860. Tom had worked for the Grand Trunk Railway since November. Every morning at a quarter after six the train blew its whistle on the Canadian side of the river. That was a signal for Tom. It was also a signal for the ferryboat. The train was ready to come across the St. Clair River.

By the time the train had crossed the river to Michigan, Tom had dressed and eaten breakfast. Mrs. Edison fixed him a big breakfast every day. Sometimes Tom forgot to eat lunch in Detroit. Mrs. Edison knew this, and she made sure that he had enough food to last all day.

Tom sold newspapers and magazines on the train. He also sold candy, ham sandwiches, and peanuts.

Most people kept their baggage with them in the coaches if it wasn't too large. Only one half of the baggage car was used for trunks and for mail. The other half was a smoking car. Since there was no way for fresh air to blow tobacco smoke out of the car, travelers didn't like to sit in there. Tom kept his newspapers and his candy and peanuts and sandwiches in this part of the car.

He reached Detroit at ten in the morning. The train didn't leave to come back to Port Huron until four-thirty in the afternoon. That left Tom a lot of time in Detroit.

"What do you do in Detroit, Tom, between trains?" the conductor asked one night on the way back to Port Huron.

"I decided to read all the books in the library,"

Tom told him. "Then I would know everything in the world. I went into the library and measured one of the shelves. I thought I would read a foot of books a week."

"Have you?" the conductor asked.

"Yes, since November," Tom said. "But I don't seem to make much progress. The library is always adding new books.

"Finally I decided I would read only books about science. It isn't hard to read a foot of them a week. There are not so many new books on science coming in all the time."

"What else do you do?"

"Well, sometimes I go to the Detroit Locomotive Works."

Here Tom had made friends with many of the men. They let him go into the workshop. He watched them make parts of locomotives. He saw the big furnaces where the men put the huge sheets of metal. The sheets got so hot in the furnaces that they came out white with heat. Tom never tired of watching the men at work.

Tom had found a good hotel where he ate his lunch. Many men ate at Finney's Hotel. At first they didn't talk much to Tom. They thought he was too young to be working on a train. Tom had begun to grow pretty tall by this time, but he was still very thin. It was hard for men to believe that he was really thirteen.

Before long, though, they began to respect Tom. They admired him because he was so energetic. They thought it was very unusual for a boy so young to work so hard. They admired him because he read so many books. He always had a book or a newspaper with him at lunch.

There was a great deal in the newspapers about the civil war everyone feared would come. Tom thought it was very sad that people of the United States had to fight one another. It seemed as if two separate countries were forming in the

United States—the North and the South. Some of the Southern states did not want to be a part of the great union. They wanted to secede and have another government. They could not agree with states in the North.

Tom noticed, after he had been eating at Finney's for several weeks, that there were usually some Negroes eating in one of the back rooms. He had been reading lately in the papers about the underground railway. He guessed that these Negroes had run away from the South and come north on the underground railway. Tom knew that it wasn't really a railway that ran under the ground. It was just a name for the secret way the slaves traveled.

There were white families all through the country from the South to the North who helped the Negroes travel to Canada. The Negroes knew which families were friendly to them. When they came to the home of one of these families, they could hide there safely through the day. They would have food and a place to sleep.

The next night the Negroes would travel on farther north. Finney's Hotel was the Detroit "station" on the underground railway. The

Negroes were given a meal there. Sometimes it wasn't safe for them to cross the river into Canada right away. Then they stayed all night at Finney's. When they finally reached Canada, they could live free lives.

All the men who ate at Finney's were interested in these slaves. They talked a lot about slavery. They said that if there was a civil war the slaves would probably be set free.

They hoped Abraham Lincoln would be the next President of the United States. They knew that Lincoln wanted to keep all the states in the Union. He also wanted to set the slaves free. The plain people all loved Lincoln. The men at Finney's Hotel loved and believed in him. Tom believed in Mr. Lincoln, too.

The months since November of 1859 had been exciting ones for Tom. He had begun to grow up. He was talking to all kinds of people and remembering everything they said. Every day on the train he read newspapers. But with all of this, he hadn't forgotten his laboratory.

Tom had two hundred bottles in his laboratory now. He made many kinds of experiments. Every time that he read about any new experiment, he went to the chemist's shop in Detroit. It was a much bigger shop than the one in Port Huron. He could get almost everything he wanted in the Detroit shop.

By the time Tom had told the conductor all the things he did in Detroit, the train had stopped at Port Huron and had started up again. As it slowed down to meet the ferryboat at the St. Clair River, Tom was ready to jump off.

James Clancy met him at the edge of the Fort Gratiot woods, and they went home together.

The Laboratory on Wheels

"I DON'T know whether Mother and Father will let me, Tom," James said.

"You're thirteen," said Tom. "You are old enough to start earning your own living."

The day before, the stationmaster at Port Huron had told Tom that the next week there would be two new cars added to the Grand Trunk Railway. One was to be half coach and half smoking car. The railroad men had finally figured out a way for the smoking car to get enough fresh air. The smoke would be blown out the windows and would not get in the men's eyes. The other car to be added was to carry baggage and mail.

Tom had asked the stationmaster if he could use some space in the mail half of the car. He wanted to put his laboratory on the train. He didn't have enough time at home to work on his experiments. He didn't get home until ten-thirty at night.

Mr. Edison always waited up for Tom to get home, because he would bring the latest newspapers from Detroit and New York. While Mr. Edison read, Tom and James sent messages on their telegraph wire. Sometimes they had so much to say that they sent messages until midnight. Mr. Edison thought this was too late for a thirteen-year-old boy to stay up.

Tom hit upon a good idea. Instead of taking newspapers home every night, he gave them to James, who met him at the train. Then James sent Tom the news stories over their telegraph wire. Tom wrote them down in the Morse code. When James had finished, Tom read the messages to his father. It was so interesting that Mr. Edison would forget how late it was getting.

Tom and James were now expert at the telegraph keys. They took messages as fast as any person could talk.

The stationmaster had given Tom permission to have his laboratory in the mail car. Tom wanted James to help him. While James took care of the selling, Tom could work in the laboratory.

Tom went with James to talk to his mother and father. The Clancys finally decided that James could help Tom.

On a bright December morning both boys jumped out of their beds with more than usual excitement. This was to be the first trip for James. The boys had taken all the bottles and other equipment to the Port Huron station the day before.

They met each other at the ferry landing. The

train was just running onto the tracks on the Michigan side of the St. Clair River.

The boys got on the train and went into the mail car. There was a long table where Tom could put his equipment. He had a metal holder for his candle. Over the table were shelves where mail was supposed to be put. There never was much mail, so the stationmaster had told Tom he could put his bottles on the shelves.

In a few minutes the train pulled into the little Port Huron station. Tom and James jumped out onto the platform before the train had come to a complete stop. They ran into the station.

"Here are your bottles, Tom," the station-master called when Tom came into his office.

"Thank you, Mr. Farley," said Tom. He went over to the table, picked up two large boxes, and carried them into the mail car.

"Put them out here on the table, James," he said. There were so many now that the train began to move before they had half of them on the shelves.

"Oh, James," said Tom suddenly, "I forgot to pick up the newspapers and the magazines!"

Just then, as the two boys were wondering what to do, the conductor came into the mail car.

"Forget something, Tom?" he asked.

"Oh, Mr. Trent, how did you ever remember them?" Tom cried. He was greatly relieved because in Mr. Trent's arms was a huge bundle of papers and magazines.

Mr. Trent left them and Tom began to explain to James how to sell.

While James went through the three coaches selling papers, Tom worked with his bottles.

There were very few bottles marked POISON now. Most of them had chemical names neatly written on little white labels.

Some of Tom's chemicals might be dangerous, but he was very careful with them. He had to be particularly careful to keep his sticks of phosphorus in a bottle of water. If they dried out they might burn. When he looked at them in the dark, they glowed with a beautiful blue

147

light. But if the phosporus ever dried out and got too hot, it would burn very fast and set everything around it on fire.

By the time James had sold his papers and magazines, Tom had fixed up the laboratory. Then the train pulled into Detroit.

Tom took James around to show him the city. They went to the library. They visited the Detroit Locomotive Works. The two boys had lunch at Finney's Hotel.

The boys spent the rest of the afternoon looking for more chemicals for Tom's laboratory on wheels, until time for the return trip to Port Huron. They hurried back to the station where the evening papers were all ready for them to pick up. James stayed in the laboratory this time while Tom sold the papers through the train.

Tom's Own Newspaper

It was early fall in 1861, and the war which Tom had heard so much about had finally come. People in the South and in the North were fighting against one another.

Tom and James were busier than ever selling newspapers on the train. All the passengers bought papers as fast as the boys could sell them. They wanted the latest news about the war. Sometimes the news was old by the time Tom got his papers to sell. He thought a great deal about this. He wished that he could give people on the train news as soon as it came across the telegraph wires in the stations and the newspaper offices. He didn't know what he could do to help, but he wanted to do something.

One day Tom went into a stationery store in Detroit. He saw an old printing press for sale there. It gave him an idea.

"How much do you want for that printing press?" he asked the storekeeper.

"Twelve dollars," the man answered.

Tom bought the press. It had a wooden frame to hold the letters of type. Tom bought a long roller, too, and three bottles of ink.

He could hardly wait to get to the office of the Detroit *Free Press*. He had made a friend of Mr. Storey in the editor's office.

"Well, Tom, what may I do for you today?" he asked.

Tom told him what he had bought at the stationery shop.

"I want to have my own newspaper. I'll print it on the train. At each station I'll have the telegraph operator give me the latest news about the war. Then I'll print it in my paper."

"Don't the people get the news fast enough, Tom?" Mr. Storey asked him.

"No, sir. Some people didn't hear about the big battle at Bull Run until they got to Port Huron. If I'd had my newspaper, they would have had the news right from the telegraph wires."

"What are you going to call your paper?"

"The *Weekly Herald*."

"What do you want me to do, Tom?"

"Well, I need paper to print the *Herald* on, Mr. Storey, and I would like to buy some from you."

"All right, Tom, you may have as much as you need. And I want to see one of the first copies of the *Weekly Herald*."

Tom promised that he would have the first one off the press. Mr. Storey arranged to have one of the *Free Press* wagons take the paper, the press and the frame for typesetting to the Detroit station.

The train was just ready to leave as Tom leaped into the mail car and got his things on board.

James Clancy was doing all the selling now. Tom found him busy sorting the newspapers and magazines.

"James, I'm going to print a newspaper!" Tom cried.

By this time James had learned never to be surprised at anything Tom said.

Tom opened his bundles and lifted the paper Mr. Storey had sold him onto the table.

"What is this wooden thing?" asked James. "It looks like a picture frame."

"You just put these letters inside the frame this way," Tom explained. He picked out a few letters of the type and put them in the little grooves which ran back and forth across the frame.

"I'll spell out your name, James," said Tom. He put the letters in the grooves. Then he put some ink on the letters with the roller. He poured more ink on a flat piece of metal he had got one day from the locomotive works.

He rubbed the roller back and forth over the ink. Then he rolled it over the letters.

"But how will it print?" James asked.

"Just you watch." Tom placed the paper on the letters which were covered with ink. Then he put a heavy piece of wood on the paper. He pressed it hard with both hands.

"Now," said Tom, as he picked up the wood from the paper, "here is your name."

Sure enough, there on the paper was JAMES CLANCY.

James was as excited as Tom. "How did you learn to do this?" he asked.

"Mr. Storey has shown me all through the Detroit *Free Press* printing room. I've watched

153

the men print the newspaper many times. I asked questions, and now I know."

It wasn't long before Tom had his first copy of the *Weekly Herald* ready to sell. It was about the size of a woman's handkerchief. He printed war news and other news about the towns along the railroad between Detroit and Port Huron.

The *Weekly Herald* sold for three cents a copy. Many people liked it so well that they ordered it for a whole year at a time. Tom printed about one hundred copies at first. Soon he had to begin printing three hundred.

There was news about many of the men who worked on the Grand Trunk Railway. Sometimes Tom printed stories about other railways. He always gave the schedules of all the trains which left Detroit.

Every week he printed a market report. He told how much things like butter and eggs and potatoes and chickens cost that week.

He printed also the names of many men and boys who had joined the Union Army to fight in the War between the States.

As soon as the train stopped at a station, Tom would dash into the telegraph office. He read the messages which were tacked on the bulletin boards. They were news notes about the war that came in over the telegraph wires. Tom read all the messages quickly. He could tell at once which ones people would want to read. He would print these in the *Weekly Herald*.

One April morning in 1862, after Tom had

155

been printing his newspaper for several months, he ran into the Detroit station. He went right to the bulletin board to read the code message. This one told about the Battle of Shiloh in Tennessee. It was still being fought, and the outcome was uncertain.

It looked to Tom as if General Grant were losing Tennessee. He was worried. He must have the latest papers. He ran to Mr. Storey's office as fast as he could. He burst in without even waiting to knock.

"Mr. Storey, I simply *have* to have a thousand papers. I will pay you tomorrow."

"Whew!" whistled Mr. Storey. "Why so many, Tom? You usually get only a hundred."

"I'm going to send a telegraph message to every station between here and Port Huron. I'm going to tell them about the Battle of Shiloh. Many people in those little towns have sons and fathers in that battle. They'll want to read about it. By the time I get to the station they will be waiting at the tracks to buy the papers."

"You may have them, Tom, and don't worry about paying me now."

Tom thanked him and went back to the station. The telegraph operator in the Detroit station was a good friend of his. He let Tom send messages to each town between Detroit and Port Huron.

Tom took his big bundles of papers to the train. At the first station he and James saw a large group of men and women standing on the platform. The boys sold a hundred papers there.

At the next station there were even more people, and the papers sold even faster. At the Smith's Creek station Tom got off the train because there was such a crowd. Everyone wanted to know about the Battle of Shiloh.

Tom was so busy selling papers that he didn't notice the train had begun to pull out.

"Wait for me!" he yelled. He ran after the train. His arms were still full of papers.

The conductor heard Tom yell and ran to the rear platform. Tom reached up his hands for the conductor to pull him up. The conductor grabbed at Tom and at the papers. He got most of the papers but let go of one of Tom's arms.

The train was gathering speed. "I'll get you yet, Tom," the conductor shouted. Then he grabbed the boy's head by his ears and gave a big pull. Tom heard a funny cracking noise in his ears, but he was so glad to feel the train under his feet that he forgot the noise.

"Here are your papers, Tom."

"What did you say, Mr. Phillips?" asked Tom. "I didn't hear you very well."

"I said here are your papers."

Tom gathered up his papers and went into the mail car. He didn't say anything to James, but he could hear a peculiar ringing in his ears.

From that time on Tom Edison was partly deaf. But it did not bother him very much right away. At the next station, Port Huron, he sold all his newspapers. People almost got onto the train in their eagerness to hear the latest news about the war. He sold the last twenty-five papers for thirty cents apiece.

An Explosion

"COME HERE a minute, Tom," called the conductor, as he stuck his head in the mail-car door. "There's a man out here who wants to see you."

Tom was working at his laboratory table, mixing chemicals in a test tube. He had just come back from selling his *Weekly Herald* and he did not want to be bothered. He did not have much time to work in his laboratory.

"Hurry, Tom. This man is from England and he wants to talk to you about your newspaper," the conductor said.

"I'll be there in a minute, sir," said Tom. He laid his chemicals down and followed the conductor into the coach. He led Tom back to a tall man sitting at the end of the car.

"Tom, this is Mr. George Stephenson. Mr. Stephenson is an engineer from London. He is studying American railways."

"How do you do, Mr. Stephenson?" said Tom, shaking hands with the big man.

"So you are Tom Edison, the editor of the *Weekly Herald*, are you?"

"Yes, sir."

"Sit down, Tom," said Mr. Stephenson. "I think that this is one of the finest papers I've ever seen. It is no wonder that everyone is so eager to buy it. You're doing a grand job."

Tom smiled and thanked him.

"How old are you, Tom?"

"I am fifteen, sir."

"Fifteen. That is rather young to be printing your own newspaper. And the conductor tells me that you know the Morse code."

"Yes, sir," said Tom.

"I believe that this is the only newspaper ever printed on a moving train. Will you do something for me? I'd like to have you print one thousand copies of the *Weekly Herald*. I want to buy them and take them back to England. Do you think you can do that?"

"Oh, yes, Mr. Stephenson," answered Tom. His gray eyes were bright. "I'll have them for you tomorrow."

"I realize this is rather short notice. If you plan to get that many papers printed in one night, it will mean hard work for you. But I shall be very happy to get them at my hotel in Detroit tomorrow."

Tom asked James to help him print the papers. The two boys did not even go home to sleep that night. They worked the rest of the day and almost all night printing the papers for Mr. Stephenson.

162

The next day, when the train pulled into Detroit, Tom was ready to deliver the papers.

Many months later Mr. Stephenson wrote to Tom from London. He told him that one of the greatest newspapers in England, the London *Times*, had printed a story about Tom's *Weekly Herald*. It had even quoted parts of it. Mr. Stephenson sent Tom a copy of the *Times* in which the story appeared. Tom was very proud of it and carried it around with him.

A few weeks after Tom met Mr. Stephenson he was again working one day in his laboratory. The train was nearing the Mt. Clemens station. He felt the train rock and knew that it was running over a bad piece of track. Suddenly the train jerked more than it had ever done before.

Before Tom realized it, all his chemical bottles were thrown to the floor. The bottle in which he kept sticks of phosphorus broke. They rolled across the floor and struck a metal band around

163

the inside of the mail car. As the sticks of phosphorus were scratched by the metal they burst into flame. Tom grabbed a bucket of water which stood in a corner of the car and threw it on the fire.

The car filled with smoke. Suddenly the conductor appeared at the door. "What is all of this smoke doing in——"

"I'll put it out, Mr. Phillips! I have it almost out," cried Tom frantically.

Mr. Phillips picked up Tom's coat and began to beat out the flames. Finally there was no more fire, but the conductor was very angry.

"This is just about enough, Tom Edison! I knew that this crazy idea of yours to experiment on the train would lead to trouble. Well, I'm not going to let you take any more chances on this train. This is your last trip!"

The train pulled into the Mt. Clemens station. Mr. Phillips pushed Tom roughly to the back door of the mail car, and threw him out on the tracks. Then he threw his bottles and his printing press after him.

"Don't you ever let me see you again, do you hear?" he yelled to Tom.

Tom was too dazed to answer. All his equipment was spread out on the tracks around him. Most of it was broken. Tom had worked hard to get all the equipment he needed for his laboratory. It would take years to replace all that had been broken. Tom was sick at heart.

Mr. Mackenzie, the stationmaster, helped Tom up, and together they picked up the bottles and the printing press. "Don't you worry, Tom," said Mr. Mackenzie. "You'll get back on the train."

Mr. Mackenzie was right. Tom went home that night. On the way he decided that he would go to Detroit the next morning and talk to the stationmaster there. After many promises that he would not take his laboratory with him, Tom finally got his job back.

One hot August day Tom got off the train at Mt. Clemens. He always liked to talk to Mr. Mackenzie, because he operated the telegraph wire. Often Mr. Mackenzie let Tom take down some of the messages for him.

Just as Tom got off the train and was crossing the tracks, he noticed a boxcar moving down the incline toward the station. It was coming faster and faster. It was not attached to any locomotive. It was a runaway car!

Tom looked along the track down which the boxcar was speeding. There, sitting in the center of it, was little Jimmie Mackenzie, the stationmaster's two-and-a-half-year-old son. Jimmie was playing in the gravel between the rails and did not see or hear the boxcar coming.

It was drawing closer and closer to him.

Tom dropped his papers and ran up the tracks.

The car was almost upon the little boy. Tom reached down and grabbed Jimmie's arm. He pulled him up and away just as the boxcar rushed past them. It came so close that it brushed Tom's heel as he jumped. The bump knocked Tom down. But Jimmie was safe, and Tom had only a few cuts on his hands from gravel.

Mr. Mackenzie came running out of the station. "What happened, Tom? Are you hurt? Where's Jimmie?"

Tom got slowly to his feet and began to brush dust from Jimmie's suit. "He's all right, Mr. Mackenzie. He's only a little bit scared. Just as I am."

"Tom," said Mr. MacKenzie, "I don't know how I can ever thank you enough for saving Jimmie's life. I'm not a wealthy man, so I cannot give you any money, but I will teach you all I know about telegraphy. Then you can help me out here at the station. You can do that between runs on the train."

"Oh, Mr. Mackenzie, I wouldn't want any money. I'd rather have you teach me telegraphy than anything else in the world."

"Then we will begin right now, Tom."

Tom worked for Mr. Mackenzie a little each day. Then the baggageman, Mr. Sutherland, said he would bring the papers to Mt. Clemens for Tom. That would save him a daily trip from Port Huron and give him more time at the station. He began to stay there all night.

Mr. and Mrs. Edison missed Tom, of course. But when he explained why he thought it best to sleep at the station, they understood. They knew that he meant to spend every possible moment working, and working hard, at telegraphy. Even though Tom was only fifteen he knew exactly what he wanted.

On Tom's trips to Detroit now he spent all his spare time at the Fisher and Long Gunsmith Shop. There he made a fine telegraph instrument. When it was finished he took it to Mr. Mackenzie.

Mr. Mackenzie looked it over carefully. "This is good work, Tom. To think that just two months ago you had your fifteenth birthday— and now you've made a real telegraph instru-

170

ment! If you keep on working as hard as this you'll have no trouble making your way in the world.

"Now I've something to tell you. Jack Ashley, who used to help me with the messages, has joined the Union Army. I'll need someone to take his place. It will mean hard work for many hours each day. Sometimes you may have to work far into the night to get all the coded messages that will come through.

"If you're willing to do this I'll be more than glad to give you the job. What do you think?"

"I don't have to think about it, Mr. Mackenzie. I'll take it and I'll begin this very minute!"

Tom Edison had his first important and responsible job! He was the happiest boy in the world.

"Moving" Pictures

"HURRY, Tom, or we'll be late for the——Tom Edison, what are you doing?" asked James in a shocked voice.

"I'm cutting out paper dolls." Tom looked up at his friend with a twinkle in his eyes.

"I never heard of a man old enough to have a job, spending his time cutting out paper dolls." James had a disgusted look on his face. "Put them away, Tom, or we'll be late for the Wild West Show."

"Please, James, just one minute. It's an experiment," said Tom, as he completed a row of paper dolls. He put down his scissors. He had folded the paper so that the dolls' heads were attached. Now five of them stood alone. They were holding hands. They looked ready to dance right off the table.

Tom was in the Mt. Clemens station. James had hurried down to meet him. The Wild West Show was at Port Huron. Everyone in town would be there.

"Now watch me make these paper dolls dance," said Tom.

"I'll watch, Tom, but please put on this dance in a hurry." James had learned by this time that nothing would stop his friend once he had started an experiment. He sat down on a stool.

Tom placed an empty water glass right by the row of paper dolls. Then he took down a piece of silk from a shelf near his table.

"What are you going to do with the silk?" James was beginning to get interested.

"You just watch." Tom began to rub the piece

of silk up and down on the outside of the glass. He rubbed very hard and very fast.

"I don't see a thing. The paper dolls aren't dancing," said James.

"Look now! Hear that crackle?" Tom asked excitedly. "That's electricity!"

Sure enough, James could hear a faint crackling sound. Then, as if Tom had commanded, "Dance!" the paper dolls began to jiggle. The electricity in the air made the paper move. The dolls jumped faster and faster until they fell over.

"You see, James?" cried Tom, as he sprang to his feet and began to dance around his laboratory. "I told you! I told you!

"James, if we'd had some way to keep those sparks of electric current when we made our telegraph, we would never have had to buy any batteries."

"What do you mean, Tom?"

"Those sparks would have given us electric

current. We wouldn't have needed the dry cells in the batteries. Well, come on. The dance is over. And I want to see that Wild West Show."

The two boys hurried out of the station. They hitched old Roman to the buggy and drove into Port Huron. The roads were crowded. People were coming from all the little towns to see the show. There were men, women, and children of all ages, and all were rushing to get seats.

As the boys tied Roman to a hitching post,

they could hear the barker call, "Ladies and Gentlemen, this way to the great show! Eighteen thousand feet of canvas! Each foot a beautiful picture! Step right this way!"

The show was about to begin. People were sitting on boxes and on the grass. A few had brought their own chairs. Many were standing. James and Tom went up to the very first row. They sat down on the grass.

In front of them were two trees about eight feet apart. To one tree was fastened a great roll of canvas. It would unwind before the crowd's eyes.

On each tree was a huge crank. There was a man to turn it. As the men turned, the pictures passed slowly from one tree to the other.

"I think it's ready to start," James whispered. "Look, the men are beginning to turn the cranks."

Everyone grew quiet. The canvas began to

unroll, and men, women, and children watched with interest. Soon they saw printing:

PANORAMA OF THE GREAT WEST

PICTURES FROM NEW ORLEANS TO LAKE MICHIGAN

The canvas moved on. Then began eighteen thousand feet of the most exciting pictures Tom and James had ever seen. There were pictures of the streets in New Orleans. Men and women were hurrying in and out of the houses.

As the canvas unrolled, there were pictures of boats going up and down the great Mississippi River. There were Negroes picking cotton in the cotton fields.

Now Tom and James were looking at pictures of beautiful mountains, some snow-topped.

But the most exciting part showed an Indian fight. There was a picture of an Indian village. It looked quiet and peaceful. Suddenly it seemed as if hundreds of Indians came running into the

village. They shot arrows from their bows and screamed and yelled.

The women and children in the audience screamed and yelled. Tom and James laughed to think that women could be so excited by pictures. They themselves weren't a bit afraid.

The pictures went on and showed a great prairie fire. Flames shot high into the air.

After the prairie fire came pictures of Lake Michigan. Then the Panorama of the Great West was over.

Tom and James walked slowly away from the grounds.

"I know you have an idea, Tom," said James. "What is it?"

"How do you know when I have an idea?"

"Why, that's easy. You always pull on your right eyebrow. Before many years, if you keep on having all these ideas, you won't have any eyebrow left! What's this one?"

179

"I was just thinking that there should be some way to make the canvas go so fast it would seem that the people and the boats on the rivers and lakes were really moving."

"How would you do that, Tom?"

"I don't know exactly. I think I'd use a much smaller piece of canvas. Then I would have to make a lot of pictures showing each little movement a person makes. When the canvas strip was turned, the little pictures would go so fast it would look almost as if the person were moving. Do you see what I mean?"

"I think so, but it would be pretty hard to do. Why, they would really be moving pictures, wouldn't they?" James asked.

"Yes, but there ought to be an easier way. If only I could make pictures of the people we see every day. They are already moving. They wouldn't have to be posed especially for the pictures."

He paused, thought for a little while and then went on. "James, I do wish I could think of some way to make pictures of people and their horses and boats and trains just as they are—moving." Tom had a faraway look in his eyes.

"I'm going home now and think about this. I have an idea. I'll see you tomorrow. Good-by!" Tom started to run toward Roman.

"Good-by, Tom!" said James patiently. He was used to having Tom leave him suddenly for an idea or an experiment.

Light's Golden Jubilee

AFTER Tom and James, back in 1862, had seen the Panorama of the Great West, Tom had begun to work on an idea for making moving pictures. But always there were other ideas crowding that one to the back of his mind.

In all his spare moments at the Mt. Clemens station, Tom worked on his inventions.

In a few months Tom had learned all there was to know at Mt. Clemens. Mr. Mackenzie helped him find a job as a telegraph operator in Port Huron. Then he worked as a telegraph operator in many large cities in the Midwest.

When Thomas Edison was twenty-two he

went to New York City. There, with two friends, he started a firm of electrical engineers. He stayed until he had saved enough money to buy his own workshop.

Then Tom moved to Newark, New Jersey, and opened his own machine shop and built his first real laboratory. He had begun his active career as an inventor. He continued to work hard and long at whatever he did.

Thomas Edison's workshop at Newark grew and grew. Then he moved to Menlo Park, New Jersey, and opened another workshop and another laboratory.

In this new laboratory he spent most of his time working with electricity. Francis Jehl and many other men assisted him.

One day in 1879 Mr. Jehl and one of his helpers were talking in the laboratory. Mr. Jehl picked up a little glass bulb from the work table.

"Would you ever have thought," he said, "that

a small piece of glass like this could turn night into day?"

"Mr. Edison has changed the world with this light bulb," the helper said.

"There were a few light bulbs before," Mr. Jehl went on, "but they burned out as soon as they were lighted. This one will stay bright for hours."

After a moment Mr. Jehl asked, "Do you remember the night Mr. Edison finished the phonograph?"

"I surely do," answered his helper. "Why, we stayed up all night to hear 'Mary Had a Little Lamb' played over and over again. No wonder that all over the world Mr. Edison is called the 'Wizard of Menlo Park.'"

Invention followed invention. Two of them did much to change the life of the world.

People wanted to talk to their friends at a distance. They appealed to Edison to help make this possible. He took a machine that Alexander Graham Bell had begun to work on and perfected the mouthpiece of the first telephone.

People wanted to see moving pictures. They were filmed with the camera invented by Thomas Edison. He had been thinking about it all those years since the Panorama of the Great West in 1862.

Thomas Edison made many friends during his long, useful, crowded life. One of his best friends was Henry Ford.

For many years Mr. Ford had been gathering material which would show how people used to live in the early days of our country. That was the way he liked to study American history. He and Mrs. Ford collected spinning wheels, whatnots, grandfather clocks, all sorts of pioneer furniture and utensils. They bought music boxes and antique chairs. Mr. Ford found some old threshing machines.

To store all these things he built houses and workshops, just like ones that Americans lived and worked in many, many years ago. They began to look like a little town. Mr. Ford called it Greenfield Village.

Because Thomas Edison was his good friend and because Edison had done so much for science, Mr. Ford decided to move Mr. Edison's laboratory and workshops to Greenfield Village. They belonged to American history.

He built a little street for the five buildings that were brought from Menlo Park, where Thomas Edison had done his first work on the light bulb.

At the end of the street stood the little brick station from Smith's Creek. It was the station where Thomas Edison had almost missed the train and the conductor had pulled him aboard by his ears.

There was also the station of the Grand Trunk

Railway. Mr. Ford moved it brick by brick to Greenfield Village, and rebuilt it.

Several of the buildings in which Mr. Edison had worked had been destroyed, but Mr. Ford built them over again to look just as they used to. He even had some soil from New Jersey brought to Greenfield Village. It was red clay.

Inside the laboratory and the buildings everything was exactly as it had been at Menlo Park. In the laboratory were Edison's testing tables. Overhead were the gas jets which lighted the rooms.

Upstairs it looked as if Thomas Edison had just left the workshop for a few minutes. The table tops were covered with bits of wire and other materials. On the wall was the first telephone Edison had helped to perfect.

On a table under the telephone was the phonograph. Near by was Edison's first patented invention—a vote recorder.

The Edison buildings were all in order by October 21, 1929. Then Henry Ford invited many of Thomas Edison's friends to Greenfield Village for a celebration.

On that date fifty years before, Edison had completed his greatest invention—the light bulb. A fiftieth anniversary is a Golden Jubilee.

Some of Mr. Ford's guests rode to Greenfield Village on a train. It was exactly like the one on which Thomas Edison had sold his newspapers back in 1860.

On the way Mr. Edison pretended to sell his wares again.

"Evening papers! Magazines! Candy and popcorn!" called the tall, white-haired man, as he walked through the wooden coaches.

"I'll take a copy of your *Weekly Herald*, Mr. Edison," said a man sitting on one of the little benches. He was President Herbert Hoover.

The people all smiled and talked about the

188

great man who was acting out his own boyhood. Thomas Edison was now eighty-two years old.

After the guests had seen everything in Greenfield Village, they gathered in a large building. Mr. Ford had ordered a grand dinner for them.

They were so placed that everyone might see the table at one end of the room. There Mr. and Mrs. Edison had the seats of honor.

Famous persons from almost every country in the world were at that dinner. Some of them were scientists and inventors. Many made speeches to tell how much they loved and admired Thomas Edison. Kings and queens sent cables to praise his great service to mankind.

After dinner the guests went to the second floor of the laboratory. It was almost dark there. The only light came from the gas jets on the ceiling.

Everybody was quiet and waiting. And all across our country men, women, and children

190

were quiet and waiting, too. They were listening to their radios—radios which Edison had helped make as fine as they were.

Thomas Edison sat in an armchair. His assistant Francis Jehl stood on a stepladder. He was ready to bring a small glass bulb to life. It had no air in it, but inside was a piece of cotton sewing thread which had been carbonized and was in the shape of a horseshoe.

"Go ahead, Francis!" Thomas Edison ordered.

Edison got up from his chair. Francis attached the glass bulb to a circuit, and the light began to grow brighter and brighter in it. The whole room grew bright. Then all the electric lights in the room came on.

Something like this happened in thousands of homes throughout the country, where people sat listening by candlelight to the celebration. As soon as they heard the announcer say that the lights had come on in the Greenfield Village laboratory, they blew out their candles and turned on their electric lights.

This was light's Golden Jubilee.

Since 1879, millions of little glass bulbs have come to life. They have spread a light as bright as sunshine and pushed darkness back into the far corners. The miracle is due to Thomas Edison, the great inventor. He worked hard and long to make the lives of his fellowmen happier, brighter, and more abundant in many ways.